Jake's Book

Book III of The Princess Gardener Series

Jake's Book

Book III of The Princess Gardener Series

Michael Strelow

OUR STREET
BOOKS

Winchester, UK
Washington, USA

JOHN HUNT PUBLISHING

First published by Our Street Books, 2018
Our Street Books is an imprint of John Hunt Publishing Ltd., Laurel House, Station Approach,
Alresford, Hants, SO24 9JH, UK
office@jhpbooks.com
www.johnhuntpublishing.com
www.ourstreet-books.com

For distributor details and how to order please visit the 'Ordering' section on our website.

ISBN: 978 1 78904 232 0
978 1 78904 233 7 (ebook)
Library of Congress Control Number: 2018955010

A CIP catalogue record for this book is available from the British Library.

Design: Stuart Davies

UK: Printed and bound by CPI Group (UK) Ltd, Croydon, CR0 4YY
US: Printed and bound by Thomson-Shore, 7300 West Joy Road, Dexter, MI 48130

We operate a distinctive and ethical publishing philosophy in
all areas of our business, from our global network of authors to
production and worldwide distribution.

Other Books by Michael Strelow

The Princess Gardener
(Our Street Books: 978-1-78535-674-2)

Some Assembly Required
(Roundfire Books: 978-1-78535-627-8)

The Moby-Dick Blues
(Roundfire Books: 978-1-78535-701-5)

Chapter 1

When Jake's parents called him and he didn't come, they always went outside and began looking for him in trees. He had his favorite trees. They looked there first. But in the spring through the new leaves and higher than anyone— especially his mother—cared to imagine, Jake climbed his favorite maple so that he balanced rather than clung there at the top, so high that he could get his small hand completely around the sliver of a branch that held him. From there, only one step and he could be in the sky, turning blue and wafting wherever the wind took him. From there he could see all the distant business of the farm: the plow waiting at the edge of the field with its impatient horses puffing and his father wiping sweat from his forehead; his sister, Alyssa, burrowing into the soil of her garden like some dark-haired mole wearing clothes like moles did in children's books; and far off, just poking over a hilltop, the castle that lolled on its own hilltop as if it too were ready to spin off into the sky and then skip like a giant stone across the lake beyond. For Jake the world was delicious from up here. It was freshly buttered bread, and it was warm pie.

When he had to come down—they would see him eventually by circling the tree trunk and spying him there at the top—he felt heavier as if each branch growing thicker as he came down also made him feel thicker and droopy with the pull of the earth. On the ground he had hungry pigs to slop, manure to fork out of the barn into a cart, leather to oil, an older sister to fetch for. And there was school. But not yet. There would be the long summer. And now with school far away as the dirt heated up with spring sun, hedgerows sang him songs of wild birds, and fancy snakes called him to come and see how beautiful they were sloughing through the dappled grass. Jake once presented his sister a complete snake skin he found, thinking she too would see the absolute marvel of it, the joy of the skin with the snake gone, the way the light shone through it and made gold. Alyssa patted his head. She saw how the gift pleased him, though she was not fond of snakes herself. And so she helped him decorate a fence pole with it where she could see it at a distance. And she thanked him with a kiss on his head.

Spring on the farm was the time where everything grew and fattened up and new, small things were everywhere. Jake was especially fond—if he had to be on the ground at all—of eating from his sister's garden. The tiny peas, so small that the flower they came from was still clinging to the pod, he snatched up and nibbled at like a rabbit. The squashes tasted best, he thought, just after the big flower fell away. In Jake's mind, vegetables excelled as food if they were tiny. As they grew, they seemed to gather flavors and fibers and smells that seemed completely unpleasant. Where did they get those from? Why didn't everyone eat baby vegetables?

And Jake had a secret. He kept it close to him, and sometimes this secret felt like it had weight and size and even made tiny noises. The secret was like a pet or even like a spider in a web that could be visited each day to see what the spider had eaten. The secret was that his sister was not his sister. She was a princess who had agreed to change places with his real sister because... Well, that was complicated. But the girls had worked out a flawless switch with only two problems: one was that Jake knew, and two was that someone at the castle also knew. There were, it turned out, good reasons why both these knowers went along with the girls' plans. But especially for Jake, the swap worked out wonderfully. He kept the secret. His sister who was just over there digging in the dirt with a smile on her face, his *new* sister whom he liked to think of as Alyssa II or too, she was actually an *improvement* on his original sister. Kinder, better natured, easier to make laugh, sweeter altogether, this was his new sister. Who wouldn't like an even better version of a sister or brother? The same only better! Everything about it was to like. Nothing about it was at all unpleasant. And at eight years old, Jake found there was not too much that could be improved in his world, but his sister was one little thing. And that's exactly what happened.

Jake loved watching a fire catch, the small flames at first from the tiny dry twigs, then the darkening of the bigger branches and the flame always reaching upwards. Maybe it was that gentle flying up that caught his attention so. Like his tree climbing. He'd watch the reach of flames, the sparks hurrying away up the chimney and smile. And so, just as soon as he was old enough, his father and mother had put him in charge of lighting the fire that would last all day and well into the night. He learned to bank the fire at night, piling ashes onto the glowing embers of the day's fire so that in the morning, he could usually just push back the ashes and begin a new fire from the old one.

With trees outside and fire inside, a sister both new and improved by circumstances, Jake could not have wanted for a finer life. Except for one small, nagging thing. Just outside the family farm, at the edge of the little woods that lead to the bigger woods, there lived an old couple in a small house with a very large garden. And, like a pair of bright birds that wouldn't sit still long enough for a good inspection, they seemed to flit in and out of their house and alight in the garden. Then they were off again while Jake swayed in the tip of his tallest tree.

The roof of their house was green like a living plant

that used the house below as a root system. And to Jake perched in his tree, it seemed the house was like those giant mushrooms that grew just outside the edge of the great woods—misty green tops with nicks taken out by some animal, tan undersides like umbrella handles stuck in the earth. Everything changed from up here, Jake thought. Gardens became patterns of color; people seemed to move slowly like each step covered only a tiny piece of ground. The birds flew by without the nervousness they showed on the ground. Even bugs high on the tree trunk were freer to be off to their bug-work and seemed happier to put one cocked leg in front of the other. When he stared eye to eye with a bug, that bug shrugged its bug shoulders and moved on, it seemed, with a bug sigh.

And so the days might have gone gloriously on like this for Jake: every day rattling with new promises, new explorations and old joys. Each day opened like a colorful flower.

The old couple, however, like the bright birds they were, just wouldn't leave Jake's mind.

"You know those old people who live just—well, over there?" Jake asked his mother one day. She had just set his breakfast in front of him, patted his head and turned to fetch her outside boots.

"Of course. What about them? Don't you bother them, Jake," she said only half sternly. "They have had sadness in their life. Best let them be."

"I know. I know. But does anybody ever talk to them? Do they like people?"

"Many of us have tried to be friendly. But... I think... I think they would rather be by themselves. They *wanted* to be by themselves after they lost their child. And then the alone part just became a kind of habit, you know. Like something they prefer without thinking about it." She stepped into her boots and stood with her hands on her hips. "It's all a very sad story. But there *is* sadness in the world, Jake. There just is, and, no, I don't know why. I don't know any better now than I did when I was your age." She paused and looked out the window and sighed. "Come with me now. We'll throw down the hay together."

Jake finished his breakfast quickly and followed his mother out to the barn. This hay business, he knew, would involve a high place in the barn, but the problem was, you couldn't see anything from in there. On the way, he glanced up at his favorite climbing tree just across the yard in front of the house. It was a sturdy silver maple that tapered toward the top into a spire like the pointy part of a castle. He could scramble up the tree so fast now, even if the branches started higher than he could reach. He would run toward the tree, and with two quick clawing motions dig into the bark and arrive at the first branch as fast as a squirrel.

Jake loved squirrels like other boys loved dogs. Squirrels knew trees in ways that Jake appreciated. They could climb or descend head up or head down as if gravity didn't exist at all, as if they were running on a flat surface. Once Jake found a dead squirrel and carefully examined the tiny claws, the curve, the sharpness, the fierce muscles behind them. And then he looked at his own hands and sighed.

His sister, Alyssa, had come upon him there pawing over a dead squirrel.

"Jake, drop that right now." Her eyes were large, her finger shaking at him. "You'll make yourself sick. It's not safe to handle dead animals like that."

"What about the cows and pigs we slaughter," he said directly to her wagging finger.

"That's different. Those are... They're *fresh*. That's the difference. Fresh meat is—different! And squirrels are

5

wild, besides. You don't know where they have been and what they were doing and…"

"Who their friends were?" Jake knew if he could get her laughing she would stop scolding immediately. And it worked.

Alyssa snorted, "Yes. And those friends might be covered in fleas and sleeping in manure piles. Just like you would if Mother didn't keep taming you. Face it, Jake. If you didn't have us, you'd turn into a squirrel yourself. Grow a bushy tail and poop in the trees."

Ah, she said poop, thought Jake. I got the princess to say "poop." That's one star for Jake and none for Alyssa. He laughed. "I would, I know. Just look at these little claws." And he held out his dead prize to her. "They're perfect for what he does. If I had little claws, I could scramble up the side of the barn. Or anywhere. You can't tell me you wouldn't like at least a fancy tail like this one." He turned the squirrel around and shook its tail for her to appreciate.

"Yes, yes, Jake. That's all very nice. Very fancy. But if we had tails suddenly, we would have to ask Mother to make a hole in back of all our clothes for the tail to stick out. That's a lot of work. I think we should just stay with what we have for the time being. Learn to appreciate our own particular genius. You know, like planting gardens and singing songs. You don't see squirrels doing those, do you?"

Jake liked the singing, hated the gardening itself while loving the pea pods and tiny squashes the garden gave him. He sighed and went off to find a shovel to bury the squirrel. But before putting it in the hole deep enough so the dogs wouldn't dig it up, he took more time to admire the entire elegance: the fur tipped in different colors for camouflage, the eyes in just the right place to take in every twitch of its complicated world, the fine tail as long as the body for perfect balance, the whiskers for feeling the wind. What a fine thing was a squirrel. Jake thought he would like to become a squirrel no matter what Alyssa said. Even if just for little while. He didn't know then just how possible that would be.

The old couple seemed to farm on their small scale with an efficiency no other farmers could match. Everything around their small house stood taller and brighter in the spring than anywhere else. Their flowers came sooner; their vegetables burst into bloom faster. During the winter months when the land lay puckered up with cold and the snow sang sleepy songs over the earth, the old couple's house grew dark with only an occasional wisp of smoke from the chimney as if they had left the fire banked and gone away. Once a visitor had knocked on their door to see if they were doing well in the bitter cold, but no one answered the door, and the visitor left worried. But that spring, the old couple emerged from their house just as the first green tips of grass poked up in the meadow. And neighbors passing on the road could see they were moving about sprightly and doing the business of preparing their large garden. When anyone waved from the road, the old woman would wave back but the old man, it seemed, did not see the wave. Or he just didn't want to wave back. But the one wave was enough to assure everyone that they were fine again this year and going about their lives. The earliest market day in town, when most sellers only had canned beets and dried herbs and tulip bulbs for sale, the old woman would show up with small bouquets of flowers— blue bells and trillium and twinflower and dogwood from the forest. And she had small bundles of greens for salads— rocket and kale and spinach—as if she had grown them under the snow somehow. The old man never came to market.

Jake and his family on market day, it seemed to Jake,

came only to talk to other people. While his sister and mother and father all jabbered to friends and neighbors, Jake found playing with the other young children interesting only for a brief while. And then his urge started, to get above everything, to leave the earth for the blue sky and the lightness of air.

But each tree in the market square had below it a ring of stands selling wares. Without flapping his arms and flying up into the trees—a thing he tried over and over when he was very young—there was no way to get to a tree. Well, there might be if he climbed an old lady or old man, some adult anyway, then skittered up a tree. Jake eyed the possibilities. A squirrel would have no problem doing that. But for a notsquirrel like Jake, there would be a different reaction.

So he circled toward the edge of the market stalls. A high wall would have to do. Something exhorted him upward, always upward, and he skulked around the backside of the wall and launched himself in his favorite direction—up. He eased along the first level then up a series of steps the people called the rookery because crows and ravens could be found sitting up there. And then his world was fine.

In the distance, the spring fields lay crisp green and ripening, looking like his mother's quilting squares lined up as far as he could see. The trees! So many trees out there to climb. So much *up* and those new leaves hiding him, waving around him!

Below him in the square, the old woman's stall was also as bright as the spring fields. The other stalls had dried flowers and dried herbs in bunches tied up with string. But the old lady's fresh flowers were like bright lights in the gloom of the dried fare everywhere else. Jake perched as much as he could like a squirrel, paws up under his chin, thinking what whiskers would feel like if he had them, how a tail would help him balance. The rookery steps invited him higher and he accepted. The old stone powdered beneath his feet, but he didn't stop until the top step. From here he could see his mother looking around the market to find him. She had always said she would put a leash on him if he didn't stay close. He knew she would look up into the trees but not up here. The feeling of being invisible, of being just a floating eyeball taking in the whole scene became delicious to him.

Jake smiled to himself and pretended to fluff his tail having quickly come back to squirrel after the strangeness of eyeball. The market movement seemed to slow down, but it was really just that now his mother was moving faster, looking under tables and finally up in the great market tree. Her hands were on her hips, and Jake knew that was one of the signs to beware of. The other was when she began tying and untying her market apron in a kind of jerky motion. The final sign would be her sharp cry: "Jake," with the "a" held like a rising warning, "Jaaaaake," came very quickly.

He slid down the steps keeping low along the wall as he knew a squirrel would. On the lower wall he slid over the backside and to the ground, brushed the wall crumbs from his shirt the best he could and prepared for the saunter. He had just learned the word from Alyssa. He knew where she got the word—from the castle where each and every one sauntered, pretended they had no place to be and like a saint moving through the land—the terra—they sauntered. She had explained the whole business to him: the sauntering. The saint, the land.

Sometimes she came very close, it seemed, to actually talking to him about what she knew that he already knew: her princess-to-farm-girl transformation. But with each day that passed, her language and her laugh began to belong more and more to the countryside and not her royal education and upbringing. And so by agreement, they never talked about it. That made it easier for both of them. And the one time his actual sister, now bearing the name of Princess Eugenie, did come home for a while—the little swap inside the big one—he could tell immediately.

One day, there was his real sister actually milking the cow, and he came up behind her in the barn. He could see how she milked. That's what gave it away. His actual sister milked without thinking, her head resting against the great brown side, her eyes dreamy and elsewhere. She was so comfortable milking that she didn't need to think about what she was doing. Twice a day for all those years! The princess sister concentrated too hard, worked to do it well and efficiently. It showed. Nothing dreamy about that milking. And even though she was found out, there was no explanation, nothing. She nodded and smiled, waiting. But Jake had found that letting the whole swapping-places thing go made everything easier everywhere. And Jake liked easy the way a squirrel enjoyed finding a nut where none was supposed to be.

The whole sister business seemed to sort itself out in his favor. Leave it alone, he thought.

His mother spotted him and waved: hands came off her hips, apron strings hung loose; she was glad to find him so quickly.

Chapter 2

It was hard for Jake to not think about the old couple over there, just outside the farm fence, how much more interesting they were than what was on this side of the fence. The old couple had that garden with tiny pea pods calling out to him: "eat me," they called. And then there were the flowers that no other gardens had yet. Somehow that pair of old gardeners had managed to grow flowers earlier and bigger and brighter than anyone else. Jake had watched from his tree top, and they both moved slowly through the garden work as if dancing to some violin. The old man was even slower than the old woman. But somehow the garden was weed free and brilliant green while the surrounding farms were still struggling to get loose of the winter gray and brown. What were they doing differently? What kind of beautiful power was in that slow dance they did with their plants?

Jake was attracted to anything that seemed different from the daily slog of the farm. He knew he would grow up and have the farm for himself someday. But in the meantime, there was the fierce call of treetops and the old couple.

Spring grew into late spring and the whole world greened up. His sisters had fallen into their new roles effortlessly now and seemed to cover themselves over with the new foliage of their lives. Jake knew he had a short time before the work became hard: his father's raised eyebrows looking for help, glancing at the sagging fence, the chicken coop roof leaking, the leather reins needing oil. Father rarely actually said what work had to be done. He knew Jake knew. Things fell apart and a farmer's life was putting them right, and then making a living out of the brown dirt.

Jake had a week at best. The spring was racing toward the sweat work of summer when everything seemed to clamor to be fixed. Every cow and chicken wanting some tending. Why couldn't a farm run itself like the woods did? No one worked in the woods to feed the birds, tend the flowers, plant the new trees. It all seemed to take care of itself. So why couldn't a farm work the same way?

The day dawned and drew Jake out the window next to his bed and then from the roof to the ground and off to the edge of the farm. Then up one of his best trees. The leaves now hid him perfectly. And there were the old couple already doing the dance in their garden: he with a hoe, she with her sprinkling can that never seemed to grow empty. She moved from bed to bed anointing the plants and then moving on. It was a slow dance but they seemed to right-foot the earth together, then left-foot in harmony. But they didn't look at each other and didn't stop to talk. Jake thought the old woman's mouth was moving; maybe she was singing but whatever came out flew away on the wind before it could rise to Jake. He looked away to climb higher, and as he looked back down, he thought the old woman was waving to him. Or was she just pushing her hair back from her forehead?

Jake plotted his raid on their garden since they seemed to have pea pods before anyone else. He would do it in the evening, just when the old couple usually went into the house with the failing light. A lantern was lit in the house. Jake came out of his tree and into the long grass. Then closer. And again closer, sneaking up in the same way he used when he wanted to get close to the baby rabbits when they first came out of the den. Too fast and they skittered back down the shallow hole. But slow and careful, and they hopped around eating the grass just outside their safe hole.

The grass was long enough for Jake to pretend to be a snake now and slither through making the least wiggle in the long stalks. He crept closer to where the garden had to be. He couldn't see much because the light was almost gone, the grass high over his head as he crawled, and somehow the distance now seemed much greater than it had appeared from the tree top. He crawled on.

And crawled on. And crawled on. The garden had to be right here! But there was nothing but grass and more grass the farther he crawled. Finally, he decided to risk discovery and stand up to see where the garden was. He stood and found himself in an endless patch of grass; no garden in sight. What happened? How had he got lost in the dark? If the garden was nowhere in sight, where was it then?

Jake took a deep breath. He looked all around the best he could. The garden had disappeared. It was impossible. There was the cottage, the frail light coming from the window. The garden should be right there, beginning a few feet from the front steps. But all Jake could see was tall, wild grass and then more grass as far as the beginning of the woods. The cottage seemed to shimmer with its tiny light. Jake sat down, plunk, confused. Maybe if he stood up quickly he could find the garden. He tried it. No luck. And then it occurred to him that his father would be looking for him to do chores before dinner, his mother would be scouting for him to fetch firewood. Alyssa would be sent by both of them to find him, and she would make her way toward the tree where she knew he'd go if he was not in any other tree. All this came rushing to Jake on top of whatever magic the old couple had done to hide their garden from boy predators.

He scrambled then, away from the cottage, away from the grass field he knew wasn't there during the day, toward the path home, toward the world where things stayed put and in their proper places. Where a cow or garden or sister were solid and without trickery.

The next day Jake was more determined than ever to find out what happened. After breakfast he sought out Alyssa.

"Do you..." he began. "Do you think the old couple, you know the ones just over there, might be witches or something?"

Alyssa handed Jake a milking pail and nudged him along toward the barn. She had to milk cows but wouldn't mind some company, and she knew he'd come and help if she dragged out her answer a little.

"Well, Jake, I think there are lots of things to think about with those people. First, I understand from Mother that they had a great misery in their life. A sick child who then died."

"I know. I know. But that was a long time ago, wasn't it?"

Alyssa opened the barn door and was met with a gust of smell: cow, manure, hay, oily leather, and then the twitter of birds feeding in the loft on scattered seeds. She handed the other pail to Jake while she fetched the soap and water to wash down the cows before she began to milk. Jake was impatient with this whole slow business.

"Alyssa, are they some kind of magic or what? Do you think... What do you think?"

Alyssa smiled. "I think they eat small children who get too inquisitive. That's what I think. Well, not children. That is, not *all* children, anyway." Jake clanged the pails together impatiently. She continued. "I am fairly sure they eat only boy children. They're much tastier than any others. Girls, I think are perfectly safe around them." And she smiled broadly remembering her adventures with

Eugenie and the old couple, their help and the wonderful working out of an important problem for the girls.

"Aw," Jake said. "They do not. If they *do* really eat children, they probably eat boys *and* girls. In fact, I think girls are much more delicious." Jake was proud of himself and set down the pails and crossed his arms. "You can just pinch any girl and see they're much more... much more tenderer than any boys."

Alyssa added, "And boys don't smell very good."

"Yes. Hey. Boys don't smell bad. Well, any worse than girls."

"Oh, girls always smell better than boys. Anyone knows that. When you're a little older, Jake, you'll find that out. Along with many other important things. You know what?" She drew her face closer to Jake's. "I think they eat little boys *because* they smell. It gives them better flavor I'll bet. When they get roasted, I think the smell cooks away and little boys get tender and delicious." She pinched his arm and laughed. Jake rolled his eyes and ha-ha-ed his sister. But the experience of yesterday evening wouldn't go away. Some might have thought to stay away from the old couple. But not Jake. He thought he would need more spying from more trees, more sneaking up. And more of whatever magic was cooking there.

Chapter 3

The next time Jake spied on the old couple it was full daytime, just after noon and lunch and that drowsy lull that seemed to come over his father after lunch and before going back to the afternoon's work. It was a time, Jake knew, he could go anywhere high or low on the farm, and no one would be looking for him.

And what a day! There was enough wind to sway the top branches just the way Jake liked them. He could wrap his legs around the high limbs and be a bird. He could inch up the tree trunk and study the line of ants going about their ant business. And he could see a much bigger world than the family farm with its endless repairing and planting and hoeing and tending. And he could see the garden next to the cottage, the one that could come and go in the evening light like a ghost. The ghost garden. But today it sits there bright and full of spring green with flowers budding in rows and clusters. Nothing ghost about it.

The old couple were about their gardening, she there, he over by the compost pile. Jake above in the sky, a hawk to their scurrying mice. Jake felt as if he could disappear from his hawk with just a wish and be only air.

The maple leaves hid him completely, he thought. He would be a hawk, then just a hawk eyeball again, then gone. But he looked back at the ground just in time to see the old woman making a circling motion with her hand. She seemed to be calling in something from the sky. And then she circled her arm again and pointed directly at Jake. Then she motioned to the ground as if inviting him to come down into the garden.

Jake froze and tried to blend into the tree. He would become the ants. She couldn't possibly see him from there.

But again she circled her arm and showed where she hoped he might come down and land in her garden. Then out of her apron she plucked an enormous cookie and held it up and circled again.

Jake loved cookies. Everyone loves cookies, even ghost cookies from ghost gardens on a spring afternoon. So slowly he came down the tree while trying to stay on the trunk side away from the garden. And when he reached the ground, he squatted behind the tree and peeked around. There she was still holding the cookie in the air and waving it around. Jake felt like the fish he learned to attract by bobbing the worm up and down in the pond. He swam a little closer through the long grass.

The cookie swirled, the grass tickled. Then suddenly there she was somehow from all the way across the garden, right there where Jake thought he was hidden in the grass.

"It's a cookie," she said kindly. "And it's a nice cookie, if I do say so myself. My husband thinks these might just be the finest cookies in the land. I'm too modest to say so myself. But there are some at the market who agree with him."

Not much else he could do, down on his knees creeping along thinking no one could see him, and there she was going on about her cookies. And it did, indeed, look like a fine cookie. Jake briefly considered running the other way as fast as he could. But… There it was: a cookie that already had something of its own story. It was a big cookie, even bigger because the old lady was so small, and in her tiny hand the cookie loomed.

"Well," she said slowly. "Do I have to eat it myself?"

There would be no running from the cookie. But Alyssa's joke also hung there in Jake's mind. Young boys smell bad but are delicious when cooked properly. She was just kidding like she always did. Of course she was!

Wasn't she?

"My name is Mrs. Trueblood. I know your mother and father. And so it's okay for you to accept this cookie from me. I know you live just over there down the path. And, I know your sister. Actually, *both* your sisters, you know. The princess one and the one who milks your cows."

She paused to let this all sink in. Jake quickly realized that she must know everything: everything about the switched sisters, the whole wedding business, the magic flowers—everything. And there she was, holding out what looked to be a truly fine cookie right near his nose.

He took the cookie. "Thank you." A quick bite, then, "This is a very fine cookie, Mrs. Trueblood. Umm... do you eat small boys? My sister says that..."

She laughed like the tinkling of small bells. "No. Never. There's not much meat on them, you know. Now you take a nice fat mom or dad. Well, that's a different story." The laugh again.

Jake stood up bearing his cookie into the sunlit garden. Between bites he eyed the young vegetables, brushed his hand along the top of a larkspur just opening but farther along in bloom than the brilliant blue larkspur he knew down along the creek at the edge of the woods. Mrs. Trueblood followed him and pointed out her growing plants for him.

"These are, or rather, will become, very long vines, and one by one, I will lift them up onto the trellis there at the end of the bed. And the cucumbers will then hang from the trellis like beautiful green things that long to become pickles. Did you ever want to be something like that?"

Without pausing and with his mouth so full of cookie that he had to answer twice, Jake responded, "Squirrel. Squirrel." Then he swallowed and turned to her. "I would really like to be a squirrel. Just for a while, to see what it's like. I watch them run up and down the trees and I think: that would be wonderful. So, I think I would be a squirrel."

Mrs. Trueblood picked a small pea pod and handed it to Jake. He popped it into his mouth with the flower petal still clinging.

He said, "I think I would start with squirrel. Then if I could make a list I would become a bird just to see how high I could fly. Then a trout. But not for very long. The water is so cold, but they don't seem to mind, and I wonder what it would be like to eat a fat bug right off the water."

Mrs. Trueblood was listening to him cheerfully. She raised her eyebrows both at once. "Well, you seem to be a very curious boy."

"I wonder about things, I really do. Alyssa, she's my sister, says that the more things you learn about the world, the more you wonder. Something like that. She is older than me."

"I know, Jake. I know." She put both hands into her apron, and around one of the beds at the edge of the garden appeared her husband.

Mr. Trueblood carried a thin stick and tapped on the edge of the raised garden bed, feeling his way with a tap here, a tap there. His pleasant face carried a slight smile as if he had just thought of something funny. His gray hair poked out the back of his tweed cap. He stopped, took off his cap and scratched his head, replaced the cap and tapped on.

Jake found himself between the two of them in the aisle between the beds of new plants. Not a tree in sight to scamper up. "I'm mostly interested in animals, I guess. Birds, how they fly. And why. That too. But squirrels lately have my curiosity up. My sister thinks to tell me that curiosity killed some cat she knows. But I'm not sure that's true. And also I don't know of any cat killed that way. Once we had a big cat that accidently got killed by a horse. But I don't think curiosity had anything to do with that."

Jake found himself babbling on about cats and horses. But the old man and woman listened to him carefully, the old man with his head cocked the way a dog listened when it heard something no one else could hear. The old woman nodding in agreement, it seemed, about cats and curiosity.

Jake went on, changing the subject. "Squirrels, though. I wonder what it's like to be a squirrel. Their tails and all. How they balance and run on a thin branch with no problem. It's like they don't weigh anything. I found a dead one once. There was not much meat inside all that fur. But maybe that was because it had been dead for a while. I thought about trying to catch a live one to find out. But my father said not to. I'm not sure why not. But I didn't. Still, I wonder, you know. Just what it feels like to be a squirrel out on a thin branch and then... jump! Jump to the next tree and land on another thin branch. That would be some fine feeling."

Jake felt a little funny. Both of them were listening to him more closely than anyone ever had, he thought. His sister often interrupted him in mid-babble and tried to steer him to his point. His mother patted his head and gave him a quick kiss on the forehead when she was busy, and she said, "Yes, dear. That's very interesting."

Jake paused and took a breath. "Having a tail..." and here he looked behind him, "would sure be interesting. I sometimes balance with my legs when I'm swinging in a tree, just to keep myself from crashing into the trunk part. Sometimes." He realized he was just going on and on. He sighed. "But, no tail. And no little claws, either. Those would be very useful. I see the way they dig into the branches. They even leave a little mark but not enough to break the bark."

After Jake had paused and began looking around, the old man spoke slowly, in a low, even voice that didn't sound scratchy to Jake, the way some old folks' voices sounded. The old man sounded more like the slow wind through a tree, but organized somehow into words. "Jake, what if you could really be a squirrel? Just for a little while. And then change back?"

Jake saw the old woman glance quickly at the old man and raise her eyebrows and then take a quick breath.

The old man continued. "Just say, you could decide exactly how long you'd like to be a squirrel. And then that time would pass and you'd be a boy again. How long would that be? Long time? Short time?"

Jake thought about it. "Probably, the first time, I would do it for a short time. But then... but then, and I know I'd love it, I would want to do it again. And for a long time. Tree to tree, don't you know. And in the woods, up and down tree trunks. And the other squirrels! How they chase each other. I think they're playing some game I can't figure out. No rules maybe. Anyway, I'd do that. Then sleep in the top of a tree in a nest of leaves. All night! Listen to the wind. Eat an acorn. Watch the moon."

All three of them laughed at once. Jake had taken them with him into the leafy nest on a full-moon night.

The old woman produced a second cookie from her apron. As Jake began nibbling on it, he thought that a second cookie is always better than the first one somehow. The first one just gets you ready.

The old couple excused themselves and left Jake to his cookie. They retired to a far corner of the garden and Jake could see them talking quietly. A bright yellow bird that he didn't recognize fluttered at the edge of the garden but didn't come in. Something seemed to be keeping insects out of this garden too, he also noticed. He hadn't one mosquito bite since he had stepped into the garden. He was fond of using his grandfather's method of treating mosquito bites. With a fingernail, you made an X on the itchy bump, hard in both directions. Then you had to leave it alone for about a minute. Then it didn't itch any more. Anyway, it didn't itch *very much* anymore. So it worked. The cookie dwindled and Jake sighed. This is one fine cookie, he thought.

The old couple returned.

"Jake, do you think it would be allowed by your mother," the old woman started, "if you could come with us a short way into the woods where the squirrels are? We wouldn't be long, but maybe you should check with her first."

Jake held very tightly to his power to decide right and wrong. His mother had told him that the old people were long-time neighbors, good people, and just preferred to be left alone. All that information he now pondered, and then he said, "My mother, I'm sure, would be fine with going to the woods. For a short time, I suppose. Not camping there overnight. I'm sure she would not allow that." And then he wondered: Would she? Is she? Does she? But his curiosity won out. And he declared himself ready for the squirrel experiment.

The edge of the woods had a lacework of tiny paths worn into the leaves and sticks. The old woman asked him to look closely and try to guess what animal was using each path. The bigger ones he declared for the rabbits. He had a friend who set snares for rabbits and had shown him how to make a loop around the path to catch a rabbit.

The smaller ones he guessed might be mice, but he wasn't sure. Maybe a skunk or a chipmunk. But the biggest he guessed right away were deer trails. He had seen the doe and fawn come out of the woods in the evening into a grassy opening to graze.

"And the very smallest?" she asked.

Jake looked closer, then closer yet. There, on his hands and knees, he spied tiny tracks cleared of debris and tiny sticks. Here an ant. There an ant, wearing tiny highways in and out of the woods, going about their business, he supposed, just like all of us. And so were all of them, the animals and insects and even the birds. They must have their trails in the sky, their favorite ways.

A short distance into the woods, the old man seemed to straighten up and took the lead with his stick feeling the way. He had hurried along as if he could suddenly see much better in the growing gloom. The trees grew thick overhead, and Jake could just make out the squirrel activity high in the branches. He knew he could scurry up any of these trunks that grew larger as they walked deeper into the woods. Here and there an immense stump appeared where the King's woodsmen had taken a great tree for the castle fires. Alyssa had told him the castle was warmed all winter by placing very large logs in huge fireplaces and then keeping a fire burning brightly all the time. There were special servants whose only jobs were tending these fires until the castle walls warmed clear across the immense rooms. He knew on the farm they kept fires small and efficient. He banked them for the night as his mother and father had shown him, and that saved wood for another day.

The old woman stopped and pointed to a stump big enough to be a dance floor for fairies and elves. Jake imagined how the party would look. She said, "The woodsmen from the castle believe that the bigger the tree, the more the castle deserves to burn it. An interesting idea. It seems a little like thinking you could get so much cleaner jumping into a lake than you could taking a bath at home.

People come to believe strange things."

The old man stopped up ahead. The sun shot a bolt of light through the leaves now like a broom handle of yellow dropped from above. Jake held out his hand to the light and it made a perfect circle in his palm like a golden coin. The old man was standing next to a tree trunk that rose into the leaves above like a great column with no branches for as far up as Jake could see. Somehow the King's men had missed this one. Jake asked how they had missed cutting it. "They couldn't see it very well," the old woman said smiling. "Sometimes the most amazing things are the hardest to see." The old man laughed and sat on a small rock. He said, "This is a fine place. I think it will work here."

The old man set about cutting leafy thin branches from the undergrowth. When he had a big enough pile—he seemed to be seeing better all the time in the woods—he held one branch up to Jake to measure it. Or maybe he was measuring Jake. Jake couldn't tell, but he stood up straight for the measuring. The old woman was laughing to herself about something she didn't share but seemed to have to do with the measuring.

The old man spoke when he was satisfied with the length of the branches. "Now take a seat. Here on the rock. Right here." And when Jake had done that, the old man turned him by the shoulders just a little so that one of the shafts of light coming through the leafy canopy hit Jake right on the back of his head. Jake put up his hand to the warm spot and then dropped his hands to his side. Ready.

The old woman asked him if he was sure that he'd like to be a squirrel for a short while. "Oh, yes," said Jake quickly. "Absolutely yes."

Jake found it hard to sit still. The excitement of not knowing what would happen, of being a squirrel somehow, of the two old people acting like children do when they're about to do something they know they shouldn't. It all went to Jake's head like the smell of a fine soup rising up his nose. The old woman explained he was to come back when he heard the whistle. Listen for the whistle!

The old man carefully stacked the branches around Jake with the thickest part of the branch to the top, the leafy part around Jake's feet and the rock he sat on. When he had finished, Jake was inside a sort of tent made of branches with the leaves spreading around his feet. The old man said, "Now try to imagine what it feels like to be a squirrel, Jake. Think what your nose must feel like, the whiskers. And listen for the whistle. When you hear it, come back."

"Close your eyes," the old woman said. "That helps sometimes. Keep them closed and see what you see with them closed. Feel your small ears, the balance of your tail."

Jake could hear her voice and the man's voice and his own voice in his head telling him to go and be a squirrel. Maybe this was it. This was all that was going to happen. Like a game where you pretended to be something for a little while and the other person tried to guess what you were. Alyssa taught him to play a game where he had to answer questions about himself until she could guess what he was. Did he have a tail? Was he furry? Could he run very fast?

Oh, well, Jake thought. It was kind of fun anyway. He opened his eyes, and he was stretched out along a branch high up in a tree. He could see two people below, but they weren't really people, he thought. Just extra things that weren't usually there in the woods. He sat up and admired the glorious and luxurious fluff of his own tail towering over his head. He twitched it twice, quickly, just to try it out. Then he flicked it again and stretched it out behind him and felt the way it balanced his body. What a wonderful thing to have! He turned to admire it and still clung to the thin branch without effort. Everything about him felt balanced. He felt completely and resplendently at home as if the tree, the wind and his own nose and tail were all part of the same thing.

He couldn't wait any longer. He began to run along the branch without thinking where he was going. He was going, he was going, and then a jump, and he was still going on a new branch and then another branch and even when a big leaf blocked his way he quick-stepped over and through like a dance he had always known. What a dance! The tree was teaching him with its twists and turns. Then another jump. And Jake, head down, raced the tree trunk to the forest floor. He jumped off the trunk about four feet over the floor of leaves and skittered across the leaves as if they were glass. They whistled and clacked behind him in a kind of applause at his passing.

Then up a new tree. This one smelled of pine pitch that grew strong the higher he ran, past a cluster of cones, then another. Then, he was hungry. And there were cones in front of his nose inviting him to lunch. Tail up. Sit up. Snap off a cone with his front teeth and hold it in his paws. It tasted the way he felt in all his squirrel glory. He ate and ate.

Then came a whistling, at first from far away but quickly seemed closer and then maybe right in his ear. He followed it. He was being called. He followed without thinking one thing. Across the pine branch into a maple, the maple to oak and down the trunk.

"Jake. Jake. Well, what do you think about it? Did you like it? Did you have fun? What was it like?" Two voices came one then the other like taking turns in a song. Mr. Trueblood, then Mrs. Trueblood. There was the taste of pine faint in his mouth and on his breath like a minty wind coming out of his face. He took a deep breath and rattled the branches of his leafy cage. The old man was removing the branches one by one. When he had finished, before Jake could answer any of their questions, he blurted out one word: "More!"

The old couple laughed together, and she said that it was always that way the first time, but that he should rest up. It might make a person tired out.

Jake nodded yes. He was very tired but also very much in agreement with his first word. "More," he said again, this time slower, less excited. But just as determined for more.

They waited for a short time, all three of them sitting on the spacious rock. Jake taking a deep breath and smiling and then trying to explain to them what he had done while being a squirrel: tail, branch running, the smell of pine pitch, the snap of pine nut. Then the old woman looked up at the sun beams and declared it was time to go back. "Be careful standing up the first time. You have to learn your old balance a little. And, Jake, remember this. It's important. When you climb trees yourself—I've seen you—when you swing around up there, don't forget that you're a boy, not a squirrel. Don't confuse the two. I know you can remember now what it was like being a squirrel. Remember that. But don't mix the two together, because a squirrel and a boy's balance are two very different things."

"Oh, and, Jake," the old man added. "Think carefully about who you tell about this. Remember that most people will find it very hard to believe. Very hard. They'll look at you oddly, and then they'll tell someone else that you are acting very strangely. And then they will all come to you with a thousand questions and… Well, think twice who you tell. And maybe we can do this again someday."

"Someday very soon," Jake jumped in. "And don't

worry, I would rather do that again than tell anyone. That's for sure. I certainly want to do that again."

Chapter 4

Back at the Trueblood garden, Jake replayed his squirrel time in his head: the branch, the pine nut, his fine and elegant tail. He felt he would burst if he didn't tell someone, but the words of the old couple echoed in his head—think twice, think twice.

I've thought more than twice, Jake thought. And I'm thinking again. So that makes three times. Well, that makes four. He skipped along the path and felt like he had suddenly become part of spring itself. The spring in his step, the spring in the wisps of green that jabbered everywhere to everything.

Alyssa won't tell. And besides she's not really my sister, anyway. My *real* sister, she would have told my father in a minute. But this Alyssa, it's as if she wants to stay with us so much that she is willing to go along with anything. Especially if I stay quiet about the switch.

And Jake couldn't stand it a second longer. He scurried up one of his favorite climbing trees that began with a long ascending slope of a sumac tree—sort of a bush, really— and that led to a branch halfway up a linden tree with its leaves like hearts scattered in the sky. Then on to an ash tree with its run-up branches reaching high into the sky. His father had cut off a number of branches of the ash where it leaned over his field, and he told Jake that the shadow of the ash kept crops from growing, and they had to be managed. And from the branches he had cut, his father had shown Jake how to make rake handles and scythe handles. The rest he piled in the barn to dry because it lit easily to build fires.

From the top of the tree he could see Alyssa in her garden, his father at the far end of a field tending to something with the horses. But he couldn't see the old couple's garden from here. Just briefly he thought that maybe they made it disappear again. Now he knew they could do anything.

After a while he came down slowly from his perch watching how the world flattened out until he set foot again on the ground and joined his two-footed family there. Alyssa was stretching her back after stooping to plant a row of seeds.

"Jake. There you are. I was looking for you every…"

"And here I am." Jake jumped and landed as if he had just alit from a tree. "It is I, Jake himself, ruler of trees and squirrels. And speaking of squirrels, I was just one."

Alyssa clapped her hands together and appreciated the small cloud of dust she had made. "Oh, Jake, you have always been one. Ever since you were little when we had to make a leash for you to keep you from climbing up the cupboards. Mother says she checked to see if you were growing a tail. She said she fully expected you to grow fur, pop out the window and run off with a walnut from the kitchen. So what else is new?"

Jake let her go on and on. He had heard all this before. Yeah, yeah, yeah. Very funny. His real squirrel secret felt delicious inside him. Anyone would look at him and not know he had been a squirrel, but there it was inside him like a song he could sing out at any moment. But until then, he smiled to himself. "Alyssa, you tell me that at least once a week, you know. But I have a secret and you would like to know it. But I haven't decided yet if you, well, *deserve* to know it. It's a very big secret. About as big as secrets come. So I might just hang on to it for a while longer." And he spun around as if he were going off towards the house. Then he stopped. "But, I can see you are too busy for secrets like this one. Maybe when you have more time and can truly appreciate something like this. Then I might tell you."

Alyssa pretended she was not interested, but Jake could see her eyes narrow and begin to plot how to drag it out of him. She took off her gloves again. "We might have to see what tickling would do to loosen your tongue, you knave." This was how she talked when they played pirate. He could hear it in her voice. It was lower, more like a pirate. Dragged out and scheming. Jake prepared to run if she came for him. But then she straightened up. "But I have so much work to do to finish this row, so maybe later. Your little secret surely can wait."

"Not little," he blurted. Hands on his hips now, he walked back toward her. "I'm only telling you if you promise—you have to promise—to tell no one. Not even Mother and Father. You have to promise. Or otherwise, no secret. It's a big secret. A verrry big secret."

They went through the complicated promising and solemn swearing they had used before. When he had recognized her as the princess that had become his sister, they used this: hand on heart, hope to die, stick a thousand needles in my eye if I tell. The hand movements that went along with the chant were just as important. Jake's favorite part was making the wiggling fingers in front of his eyes for the thousand needles. Not bad either was the "hope to die" part with rolling your eyes back in your head to look dead. They did it twice because Jake thought the secret was important enough for two times. No mistakes. Done.

So, slowly and leaving out no detail, Jake told his sister how he had become a squirrel and exactly what that was like and how he would like to do it again soon and do it for a longer time and be a squirrel for maybe a whole afternoon and meet other squirrels too.

Alyssa listened patiently, nodding, looking down

once in a while at her chipped and cracked fingernails and absently cleaning the dirt from one. When Jake had finished and was standing there aglow with his story, she cleared her throat. "That's all very nice, Jake. But until you let me come along and change into, let's see, maybe a hawk. Yes, I'd like that. I can't really believe you until I get to be a hawk. Oh, and by the way, I promise not to eat you while you're a squirrel and I'm a hawk."

Jake looked at his sister. She was smiling so he couldn't tell if she was even taking all this seriously or just making a long joke out of it. Finally, she took him by the shoulders, looked him in the eye and said, "Jake. I know something very important happened to you while visiting the old couple. The Truebloods. Both Eugenie and I know what they can do. But we don't know how they do it. We were amazed by how they saved all the farmers who had their flowers taken for the wedding of the Beauregard clan. We thought they went away, into the woods, and would never come back. But there they are again. Right back where they were when Eugenie and I met in their garden. Maybe it's your turn now, Jake. Maybe they are there now because *you* need them now. I don't know."

Jake had never heard his sister talk like this. She always seemed to be kidding him, not talking straight so that he would figure out what she was really talking about. He would always walk away from her not knowing what had just happened, but just as surely he always walked away feeling good, like he had been playing some kind of pleasant game with her. His real sister, who now lived in the castle, was never that way. *She* was always telling him how to be, how he *should* be. While this version of his sister was much more fun. The whole sister trading had worked out so well that he not only went happily along with it, but he saw it as a fine improvement in his life.

And now! Now he felt like his regular farm life had suddenly gone through the pages of an exciting book he was reading. Now he found himself tiptoeing through the pages of an adventure that was really happening to him. The Trueblood magic. He didn't care how they did it, not like Alyssa did. He didn't care even if the whole thing was somehow dangerous, and he wouldn't be able to come back after being a squirrel. Getting stuck there and having to live his whole life there! He just didn't care.

And what occurred to Jake almost immediately was that if the old couple could make him a squirrel, then they could do anything. Anything! He could become any bird he wanted. He could be a mouse or a worm or any fat beetle he wanted. What if they could teach him the way to do it? Wouldn't that be amazing. He could sit in school and if he got tired of school, right there he could become a spider high in the corner of the room, right behind one of the big beams that held up the roof. And there he could sit in his web and wait for something tasty to come along. Then he'd feel the web twitch. Then he would slowly crawl down to see what there was to eat today. Then pounce! And sink his jaws into a fat moth. He'd spit the wings out, of course. Who eats the wings? And if he didn't feel like eating the whole thing right away, then he would wrap it up and eat the rest later.

Jake had watched the barn spiders do this work many times. He tried to poke the web with a twig to get the spider to think an insect had arrived. But it never worked. But when a real insect got caught, he watched the spider slip out of the dark corner where it waited and then come down to eat. He noticed that if he watched very quietly, if he waited and didn't move and didn't breathe right onto the web, then the spider came to feed.

Yes, he thought. Being a spider could be very interesting.

But there were mice and voles and horses and cows to be, too. Wouldn't his father be surprised if he harnessed his plow horse one morning and old Ruben turned around in his traces and neighed, "Hi, Dad," at him.

And then there would be owls. Jake knew that owls were a kind of bird, but what a bird! Owls could do things other birds couldn't, almost as if they had special owl rules for themselves. And they left behind those pellets with tiny skulls in them and hair from what they had eaten. Owls, yes. They would be so much better than those worm-eating robins that raided the haystacks. Or those blackbirds with the yellow eyes that only seemed bent on being noisy.

Jake gave in to being lost in thought while Alyssa returned to her gardening. He thought about changing himself among the farm animals: geese yes, chickens no. Horse yes, cow... well, maybe, but just for a little while. Goat, oh yes. Sheep. Well, he would have to see. Maybe that ram Old George who slammed his head into everything around him at certain times during the year. That whole business seemed so stupid that it was interesting.

But owls, yes. Oh, the nights he could get to know while being an owl. The secret of flying without making any noise at all. The other flying things to eat while flying yourself in the dark. What did a bat taste like? Were they crunchy? Were they easy to catch? How could you see them after dark? Owls, yes.

Almost without thinking about it, Jake skittered up the big maple next to the house. He was so comfortable there and knew the order of the branches so well, that he didn't really need to be careful or even choose the next place for his hands and feet. They knew where to go, and there he was—perched up in the top and not even breathing hard. What a fine place to think about the world.

Jake thought that Alyssa didn't seem to take the whole

squirrel business seriously. Or maybe she really did. She certainly knew about the old couple's powerful ways, how they could change one thing into another thing. How they seemed to be able to come and go in some mysterious way and break the rules that everybody else had to follow. Jake wondered from his airy lookout if Mr. and Mrs. Trueblood had somehow found a way to come and go from the regular world of working and cooking and eating. Like they could have both worlds, maybe. Or slip back and forth to… To where? Was the world he knew just one of many? Could he learn to do it too? What would he have to learn? Would they teach him?

Jake swayed and hummed a little. He could see his mother circling the tree below. She was getting ready to call him down he knew. Every day she said she worried more and more about his climbing since he got heavier and bigger all the time, and the tree could only support so much, and then it would break. She asked him to just not go out so far on the thin branches. Stay with the bigger branches that would hold him. But to Jake the whole point was the swaying, adding himself to the two-part thing that was the wind and the tree. As he climbed up, he felt himself mix with the wind and the tree, and there out on the skinny part—the dangerous part according to his mother—the transformation took place.

Jake sighed in the sighing wind. If he didn't do the dangerous thing, his mother would be happier. Happy mother. But then he would find himself back on the tree trunk where there was almost no sway, where the wind and the tree were two separate things. The old couple and their ways seemed to solve the problem nicely.

Of course, he couldn't *tell* his mother how he was going to solve the problem that made her so uncomfortable about his safety. But he could pretend that he was being more careful now, that he was being more thoughtful and grown up. Wasn't it almost the same thing? The wind and the swaying and sun on the leaves had no answer.

Someone he might tell about the whole thing was his real sister, who now lived in the castle. She understood danger. If anyone found out that she and the princess had switched places, *she* would be the one who would be punished with all the fury of the army and the King and, well, just about all the fury there was in the whole kingdom. The princess, who now tended his family's garden and milked the cows, she would be taken back to the castle and probably made to sit in a very fancy chair for a very long time and listen to lectures about how she could not be allowed to wander in the countryside like a commoner and dig in the dirt like a farmer. She carried the rich blood, the blood that sang the song of history and great peoples and great deeds. *She* owed the kingdom her complete attention, her complete life.

Parts of this Jake had heard all his life: the blood, the history, the castle, the realm, the one-thing-after-another. When his sister dared to take her life into danger, wasn't it like hanging there out on that thin branch swaying with the wind and becoming part of everything huge in the world? Well, he thought. It sure seemed like it. Same danger. Same delicious feeling.

His mother did call Jake down before he had time to sway himself into knowing what to do. What he did know was that he had to go back to the Trueblood garden where all things seemed possible, where squirrels and boys and wind and trees and old people all mixed together in a swirl like his mother's bread dough. He like to watch her start with dry this and wet that and then mix and knead and let rest, and then the baking and the warm bread with butter. That certainly was a kind of magic too, a magic of changing one thing into another, plain stuff like flour and water and butter into brown, steaming bread. Mrs. Trueblood was just as magical as that.

On the way down, Jake paused to watch a squirrel in another tree and smiled a secret smile known only to boys who had become a squirrel.

Chapter 5

There were night noises. There were always night noises, of course, but these were different. Jake opened his eyes and pulled the blankets up under his chin. He knew the best thing to do would be to pull the covers all the way over his head and go back to sleep. But the noises were there clearly just below the general farm noises that decorated the night. A cow would moo to the moon. A pig would scratch its back and make the pen railing sing like a musical instrument. And the chickens always had some short argument they proclaimed to the darkness.

Jake listened to what sounds were cooking just below those. A kind of rustling maybe, like when a storm wind was just beginning, and off and on the leaves shuddered at the coming storm. Or like water, Jake thought. Like there was water running somewhere that hadn't been running before and now was adding itself to the night commotion. It didn't get any louder, or any quieter either. There it was; he couldn't stop hearing it, and so he listened to hear what direction it was coming from. Finally, he had to close his eyes to hear clearly, but it seemed to be coming from the deep woods beyond the farm and next to the old couple's garden. He had walked that path into the woods to become, briefly, a squirrel. There was not one person in the world who could honestly say that very sentence out loud. Only Jake, Jake the boy-squirrel could claim that. He listened to the noise and thought how he longed to try out the squirrel change again.

He sat up in bed and looked out beyond the roof of the barn. Whatever was making this noise was not spooking the animals. A storm would set them all quacking and clucking and mooing. Even the horses would join in if the storm was of proper importance for them to leave behind their air of superiority over the other animals. But tonight they were silent, the noises rustled and burbled somewhere perfectly between water and wind, and Jake could feel that the night itself was waiting to see what would happen.

The woods, if we can fly over the barn roof and alight just at the edge, skittered with critters of all sorts chasing around in the leaves and sticks of the forest floor. But that wasn't the noise, or at least, not all of it. The old couple had come to the center of the woods, making their way by the beams of moonlight that found their way through the leafy ceiling of the forest. They stopped at the biggest tree, and as was his habit, the old man looked for some place to sit. The old woman busied herself with something on the bark of the great tree as if she were picking something there. And as she worked, the tree began to grow lighter and a sound of washing and whispering added itself to the sounds of the small animals on the forest floor. It seemed like an orchestra adding instruments: the violins, the horns, the booming bass, the sweet cellos one after another while the tree glittered as if it were collecting the beams of stray moonlight and adding them to its great trunk.

The tree melted in light. Not a door opening, but more like a door growing in the light and becoming an open door that stood wide and inviting. The old man made a small grunt when he stood and followed the old woman through the open door. And they were gone.

Jake only heard the water-wind suddenly stop, and the night returned to its usual animal sounds and an occasional night bird. Owls prowled. Mice took advantage of the moonlight to find seeds and owls took advantage of the delicious mice. And the center of the forest was quiet and soft and deep as if all the moonlight had been recently used up to power the amazing tree trick.

Jake awoke the next day to a changed world. But he didn't know it yet. Eugenie, who used to be his sister and now lived as a princess, she knew it. Alyssa, who was now his sister but used to be a princess, she didn't know it yet, but she soon would. The two girls had a habit of meeting once a month in the old couple's garden where they sat on the stone bench and traded tales of their exchanged lives. That meeting was coming up, and what Eugenie knew in the castle would come out in a rush to Alyssa who had come fresh from her garden.

Including the old couple, there were five. Jake was high in a tree surveying the countryside and keeping an eye on the garden below. The old couple worked on opposite edges of the garden. And on the bench in the center sat the two young girls who had exchanged lives, had taken turns sharing Jake as a brother, and who now felt that this garden, this stone bench, was the only place in the world where they could laugh and talk together.

Alyssa from the farm began with excited reports on her garden and spring projects. Eugenie, patient and full of news herself, waited until Alyssa was done. Each girl wore something like the costume of her place: Alyssa wore a shirt of heavy cloth that everyone called "village cloth" because it was woven nearby, and a dark brown vest on top with very large and farm-useful pockets; Eugenie wore a dress of much finer cloth with small flower decorations along the collar and a pale blue belt tied in a small bow. Each girl, of course, was in a kind of disguise, in fact *lived* a kind of disguise ever since the switching took place.

Eugenie leaned over to Alyssa and said, "You know Jake is in his tree. Did you see him?"

Alyssa laughed. "If I can't actually see him walking around, I know exactly where he is. Right up there. He's such a good brother. Thanks so much for breaking him in for me."

"I am pleased to have been of service," said Eugenie. "A brother is a wild thing, and it's important that we girls stick together in the matter of civilizing them." The girls had begun to laugh together, knowing that the subject of Jake brought out their funniest. "And," she continued, "can you imagine what a sorry world we would have to live in if girls everywhere didn't tame their brothers properly. Oh, the wild things running around causing mischief everywhere."

Alyssa glanced up at Jake's tree. "There would be large herds of these very familiar monkeys swinging about in high places."

"And always stealing food. They would never stop."

"And… and then there would be a roundup every once in a while, of course. Some could be useful on the farm. And others could be soldiers."

"Or useful for general digging and stacking. I think that a few could be trained to pull wagons."

The girls laughed together so hard that neither could speak for a minute.

Eugenie, who was always looking to the future since she had moved to the castle, continued. "And a small number might be raised to make proper husbands someday. Cleaned up, taught to eat correctly, told to stand up straight, taught not to put sharp objects in their pockets. Oh the list is endless." She rolled her eyes.

The girls cherished these stolen moments together. And here in the garden it was as if, first, they couldn't be found by either the farm or the castle, but, second, they couldn't be seen by the rest of the world passing by on the road just a little way from the old couple's small house.

When they had finished entertaining each other with the subject of Jake, Eugenie took a deep breath to change the subject. "We have to talk about Arbuckle Beauregard

The Third."

Alyssa raised both eyebrows at once. "Arbuckle? What in the world could be important about Arbuckle now that he's married and prancing around in his silly green vest?"

"Where to start?" Eugenie said, resolved to tell all. "The wedding. It was after the wedding and all the magic of the flowers and the money. Arbuckle tried to take credit for everything. You and I know better, of course. And Jake knows. And Arbuckle. But he stayed silent when others suggested that he provided all that money to all the wedding tables to pay all the farmers for their flowers. He would just smile and nod, smile and nod and let the people think whatever they wanted. And pretty soon, everyone thought the same thing. Arbuckle and his new wife's families had rewarded the kingdom's farmers on the occasion of the great wedding.

And that might have been the end of it. But Arbuckle began to believe it himself, I think. As if some magic that he didn't understand had somehow chosen HIM to lift up the kingdom. His family restored to their rightful place not just as royal cousins but as rightful heirs to the throne! Of course, he knew that I knew otherwise. And he knew that you and Jake also knew. But because none of us could stand up and say what had really happened, he was sure of our silence on the matter. And after he figured that out, then I think he actually began to *believe* it all himself. And so, what is the big deal?

Well, now Arbuckle, his wife and both their families are planning to throw out my—our—father and replace him with Arbuckle and his new heir that will come soon. Right now everyone in the castle is taking sides. The old ones think the present king is a wise and just ruler, and he should continue to rule. But there are just enough—maybe Arbuckle has promised them power if he becomes king—

just enough to make things very uneasy at the palace. Some say there will be blood. That plots are happening already. The servants don't know which side to take. Every day there are new intrigues and worrisome groups forming for or against the King. I see them like flocks of birds breaking first one way and then another, filling the sky with all their noisy squawking. But there is, I think, real danger ahead." Eugenie took a deep breath as if all this coming out in a rush had left her empty—of words, of breath.

Alyssa sat with her mouth open, not quite able to believe that her old home was in such a mess. She hated the thought of being dragged back into palace schemes and the clacking tongues of lords and ladies. She sighed. How simple and beautiful—and elegant, and useful—her garden seemed. A carrot, a bean, a beet. That was where her heart was, had *always* been.

Eugenie sighed. Alyssa sighed. It didn't matter which one was which.

Jake plotted to get his work done early so he could go see the old couple. After thinking long and hard about what animal he would like to be next, he decided that he really would like to be a squirrel again. After all, he had only been a squirrel for a short time. It seemed, thinking back, so very short a time he had traveled the treetops as a squirrel. He had barely come to know his own tail! And the whiskers, he still wasn't sure exactly how to manage them. If he tried out other animals he wouldn't get to know any of them very well. And that was when Jake decided to concentrate on knowing squirrel. He would ask them to give him a longer turn this time, like learning to add and subtract. He would study what added up to squirrel and what subtracted from Jake.

The manure flew from Jake's pitchfork. The chickens

scurried away from him as he raced through feeding and checking for eggs. Even the solitary ram, Old George, backed away from his fence as Jake raced by to tend to the stray ducks, clip a wing or two to make them stay on the farm.

Jake's cheeks were bright red and the sweat stood out on his forehead. Suddenly there was a hand on his shoulder. His father held him steady.

"Jake, you'll scare all the animals. They don't like a boy flying around like a devil with its pants on fire. It makes them all very nervous. They think something's wrong. A fox, they think. Or a bear. Take a look at the ram. He's sure wolves and pirates are coming after him any minute."

Jake took a deep breath. "I was just, seeing... seeing how fast I could do chores. I didn't know it scared anybody. Any animals."

His father laughed. "Look at the chickens. They have skedaddled into the coop like they do when a storm is coming. So I think you qualify as a storm, Jake, a boy storm."

"I'll slow down. I promise." And Jake showed how he would walk strangely like a scarecrow prancing off its stick in the corn field. He raised his arms slowly and made gestures in the air—slow, silly circles. His father laughed again and patted him on the head.

"That will be just fine, Jake. You do that. Pretty soon all the animals will stampede off the farm and make a break for any new barn they can find."

But Jake knew that once he had made his father laugh, all was well. He could do his chores any way he wanted, fast or slow, as long as they got done.

His father wandered off toward his waiting team of horses. The sun and wind took a deep breath and went about the day's business. Jake hopped up to a low branch of the barnyard shade tree but immediately swung back down. He had business to do too. Squirrel business.

Chapter 6

The late afternoon light sang with possibilities. Jake finished his chores and had nothing to do until he had to show up for dinner. Two whole hours to dig into squirrel adventure. But as he came upon the old couple's garden, they were nowhere to be found. The plants glowed, the birds and rabbits seemed to pause at their busyness, no mosquito buzzed.

The path leading into the woods had bent grass telling Jake someone had passed there not long ago. And so he skipped his way toward the forest, constantly checking the trees for squirrels. There were black squirrels, gray squirrels, and now and then a shy red squirrel.

The paths seemed more confusing this time. Jake didn't remember so many paths going in different directions. He had just followed the old woman last time. But now a path he started down just seemed to stop. So he backed up and tried another, but it too just disappeared into the sticks and leaves of the forest floor. Back again, but this time he couldn't see the path he had been on and found himself standing in one spot with no path, a few beams of light coming through the canopy of leaves, and no idea where to go. He remembered that if he got lost when the family walked, he was to stop and stay still until someone found him. But here, no one knew where he was; no one was with him. The woods seemed darker than before.

Jake listened. Where were the birds and squirrels that filled the woods when he started out? He thought he might climb a tree to see where he was, but all the trees in this place were very large and branches began so high up the trunk that it seemed impossible to scramble that high, even for him. This woods suddenly seemed very different from the woods he had been in before. It was getting hard to see anything. Up his back crept a tingling like a large, invisible insect. Or was it the sweat running down his back under his shirt? The beams of light were growing dimmer as if some giant hand were turning off the lamp. Jake sat down, plunk, on the forest floor. Something was coming and something was still coming, and he could not do one thing about it. He closed his eyes, like crawling under the covers, and for a second he felt better and then the sound started.

Far away at first, then closer like the excited call of a flying bird. The sound changed as it got louder, changed into a lower sound like the huff of a tired horse, the grunt of the pig eating. Jake opened his eyes and blinked. The light was gone, and the forest was full of low sound that had worked its way into a moan. And, Jake realized, he was suddenly very hungry. Hungry and about to be eaten by a monster, he thought. He closed his eyes and waited for the end: teeth, drooling slobber, claws, burning eyes, a whipping tail all attached to a hungry something that certainly would eat a small boy. His imagination bloomed; he held his breath. And suddenly the noise stopped: not one bird sang, not a leaf rustled.

He opened his eyes again, and there coming toward him in the gloom, followed by a kind of light that stayed wherever she put her foot, was the old woman soundlessly stepping through the woods. Jake took a quick, deep breath. He realized he had not been breathing at all while waiting for his horrible end. But there she was, smiling, holding out one hand, the other hand in her apron where the light seemed to come from, shedding itself everywhere in front and back of her.

"Jake. Come with me."

Oh yes, thought Jake. You bet. I will come with you right away. He stood up and brushed at the leaves and twigs he had collected waiting for his fate. The duff, he thought. That's what all that stuff on the forest floor was called. The duff. He was just about to be eaten by something in his own imagination, and all he could think of was his new word. The duff. The duff.

He took the old woman's hand. It felt warm and light. With her other hand she produced a cookie, also warm and light. Jake silently ate the cookie while she led him across the trackless forest floor and suddenly there was a worn path. Then another and another. The light grew, the spooky silence cracked open to include birds and skittering and the sound of his own feet in the duff. She said not one word until they came to the old man sitting on a mossy rock, smiling, eating his own cookie. And there was the enormous tree with the door that wasn't really a door. This was the squirrel place.

The old man spoke. "She can hear everything in the woods, you know." And he laughed. "Everything! She hears lost boys most of all." He looked at his wife, and she raised her eyebrows and smiled back.

Jake finished his cookie and sat on the mossy rock ready for the tent of branches. He closed his eyes and waited. The old woman's voice came slowly, clearly.

"Remember, Jake. When you hear the whistle, you *must* come back right away. Even when everything in the trees is very interesting. The whistle will tell you to come, and then you come down. Back to us. The squirrel time will be over when you hear the whistle," she said.

"I will. I will come back," Jake said quietly. He knew how to follow instructions. So many things on the farm could be dangerous, his father had told him as soon as he was old enough to listen well. So much harm could come if you didn't listen to warnings: a horse's hoof, a sharp tool, a ragged stick of chopped wood, a flying pebble, a pitchfork left hidden in the haymow. Listen, Jake. He listened. But in trees there was only the wind and his own joy to listen to. On the ground was danger.

The old man said, "We will whistle. You must come then." Jake nodded. He understood. Mr. Trueblood continued, "There will be no mistaking the whistle. It won't sound like anything else you will hear. You heard it before. Be sure."

Yes, yes, thought Jake, impatient to be a squirrel again. The old man sounded the whistle once just to remind Jake of the sound.

"Yes," said Jake.

And with only a few branches forming a tent this time, Jake was scurrying up the trunk toward the light at the top of the canopy of leaves.

He wasted no time doing the same things he had done before. He headed straight for the thinnest branches that would hold him. Higher and higher up the beech tree with its gray branches like its own forest of Ys reaching up and up. He didn't stop to sniff the young beechnuts. He felt his claws dig into the thin bark and leave a trail of his squirrel initials behind. He felt a delicious and safe hold higher and higher until one branch finally bent with his weight and lowered him to another branch and that to one more. He could scamper sideways in the tree until he had to turn and go back or try a leap to the next tree. The leap seemed impossible, he turned and ran back, sat, looked over his shoulder, past his tail and marked where he might have leaped. He decided to go up again, this time racing the biggest branches toward the top, but the leap did not leave his mind.

He thought squirrel things: the smell of new twigs. He thought boy things: I could fall but also could catch my squirrel self. He thought: what about that other tree, over there? What about another squirrel? What about the sunlight at the top?

Jake paused and felt his heart beat squirrel-fast in his chest. All things squirrel were possible. All things boy. He was like sunshine and shadow mixed together on the forest floor. He was Jake wrapped in lively fur and had a nose for anything he could eat. Again up the tree, then down, then back to the branch and without pausing a second he leaped to the next tree lower and partially shaded by the great beech. And he landed without a Jake thought. He could feel the Jake thoughts fading, getting farther and farther away.

And then the whistle. The first one was thin and distant. The second was stronger, and he knew he must run back quickly. He chose the ground, and head down rushed for the forest floor and scampered toward where he knew he had to go. And it was over.

He rested a minute. The old couple smiled but this time didn't ask how he had enjoyed his squirrel time. They took his hands, one on each side and silently led him out of the forest and into the opening just outside their garden full of sun.

Jake tried to think how long he had been gone. The sun time seemed about the same as when he had wandered into the woods. Could it be the same, no time passing? It must be later. He should be getting back to his chores, to his being careful about things on the ground. He glanced up into the trees at the edge of the woods and smiled. He knew now he had another home there as long as the old people would let him roam their forest as a squirrel. He knew that any time they would let him, he could shed his Jake-world like a winter coat on a warm day and spring into a tree-world where he felt he had always belonged.

Strange, he thought, how much bigger the woods were on the inside. He had walked completely around them on the outside, easily traipsing from field to field. But once inside they seemed endless and immense as if there were no end, no beginning.

The old woman complimented Jake on returning immediately after he heard the whistle. She asked him if he needed another cookie to feed him on his way home. He did.

And the path home was delicious too; the evening light seemed sweet on his eyes like the cookie on his tongue. But his feet felt heavy compared to his recent tree-top scampering. His tiny squirrel feet had felt like air beneath him, his furry body like the air itself as he ran along a branch high above the ground. He smiled to himself, keeping his own council of delight. Then he found, without trying, his feet began to skip along the path toward home as if they too remembered his squirrel lightness.

Just as he rounded the barn and headed toward his evening chores, Alyssa called to him. She was calling to him from inside the barn.

He peeked in the door and called back.

She said, "Where were you? I was looking everywhere for you—tops of trees too. I thought you might be hiding out in the hay away from work."

Jake's smile came back. Tops of trees is where she could have found him all right. Tops and trunks and even the slimmest of twigs.

"What are you thinking?" she asked. "I know you. You were doing something you weren't supposed to do. Weren't you?" she took him by the shoulders and turned his face toward the light from outside the barn. "Weren't you? You know you can't hide it from me for very long. I'll find out eventually so you might as well tell me now and save time. Jake? Tell the truth and shame the devil."

Jake laughed. He knew she was in a mood to fool around and anything would work, but something made him say it. The truth. Just to see what would happen. "I was practicing being a squirrel. That's all. Furry tail, little claws, run up a big beech tree in the woods." He watched Alyssa's face to see what would happen. She never changed a bit.

"And how was that, being a squirrel? Oh, you've been squirrely ever since you were born. Mother said, I remember it clearly. 'Your brother, dearest Alyssa, looks quite squirrely. So prepare yourself when you see him.' And there you were, a kind of wrinkly bald squirrel with little beady eyes making your squirrel noises right after you were born. You turned out to be a boy. Sort of." She laughed. "But it could have gone either way according to Father. He said the old stories always have children born as animals and then the family has to tend them and finally set them free. All kinds of animals too. Not just squirrels." She examined Jake's face and brushed at where his whiskers had been. "Those old stories are full of wolf-boys and rabbit-girls and even a chicken-boy I remember. We all thought you might be one of those at first. But, no. Here you are, the boy all of us hoped for." She patted his head just a little too hard.

"Well, let me tell you, sister. The squirrel life is the life for me."

"Not a pirate? I remember when you wanted nothing but to be a pirate. And then we heard about the *real* pirates taking people's food and animals. Then you changed your tune, mister. So today you were a squirrel. Tomorrow what? A June bug? Big fat June bug. I think that would be fun for a while."

Jake thought, hmm, she's certainly taking all this well.

Of course, maybe she really doesn't believe a word I ever said about being a squirrel. I'm not sure. So I'll just have to say more. "The squirrel, you know. It is a kind of king in the trees."

Alyssa glanced down at two pails just inside the barn door. "Jake, are those the pails I asked you to wash out this morning? The longer you leave that milk in them, the harder they are to clean. Just soak them for now."

"Well, I was busy, you know, with the squirrel business."

"And now you made your job harder. Do your squirrel business *after* you get your work done next time. If Father sees the milk gone bad in the bucket, he will eat both of us for dinner." She raised her eyebrows to make sure Jake knew how unpleasant it would be to be eaten by Father for dinner.

Jake sighed. "I'll clean them now. I will probably want to be a squirrel again tomorrow. And the day after. And the day..."

"Certainly, Jake. But just remember, one day you might just *stay* a squirrel. And then spend the rest of your life looking over your shoulder at every hawk circling in the sky, every marten and ferret in the woods searching for you to eat. Just be careful to stay a boy enough of the time to get your work done. Agreed?"

"Just listen for the whistle." Jake put his hand to his mouth. I didn't mean to say that out loud, he thought. Not the whistle part.

"Whistle? What whistle?" Alyssa handed Jake the two buckets.

Jake whistled the best he could an old and tuneless song that really was not very pleasant to hear. And Alyssa sighed, patted his head again and gave him a gentle shove towards the washing place alongside the barn.

Chapter 7

There was talk, his mother said at dinner, of problems at the castle that might be big doings someday soon. Everyone at the market had been worried that something was falling apart there, some kind of intrigue.

"What's an intrigue?" asked Jake. "Is it like a war?"

Father said, "Sometimes it's worse than a war. At least in a war you know what the sides are. But with intrigues, there aren't clear sides. Until, suddenly, there are."

Jake thought that his father's words cleared up nothing. "So intrigues are like pirates? Like stealing things that aren't yours?"

Father chewed and scratched one ear. "Like pirates? Humm. Maybe an intrigue is like pirates in some ways. Tell me, Jake. What do you know about pirates?"

"They take things that aren't theirs and then run off to sea in boats. I guess they sell the things they take and then hide the money. On islands, mostly. Sometimes in hollow trees. In big chests full of money so they can come back later and get the money. When they are old, I suppose. They need the money when they are old and can't work anymore at being a pirate every day. Like Mister Moore who lives behind the church. He can't work he is so old, I think. So he must have saved some money. Maybe in a chest. Maybe he was a pirate and now he just…"

"Easy, Jake. Mr. Moore used to work digging graves, not as a pirate. But your pirate idea is not too bad. At the castle there are something like pirates. You remember the flowers they came and took. Everyone's flowers for the wedding?"

Mother looked at her husband and touched her ear. Alyssa knew that meant that little people had big ears, and we should be careful what we say around them because they just might blab to the wrong people and cause problems for everyone.

Alyssa added, "Jake used to talk about pirates all the time, but I am not sure he knows exactly what pirates do, how they live."

"I do too," said Jake. "My friend Andrew told me he knew a pirate once but that pirate got killed because he stole from the wrong man and the man caught him and killed him."

"That's quite enough talk about killing and pirates *and* castle intrigues, I think," said Mother. "Let's change the subject for a little while and see if that doesn't help the food sit better on our stomachs. What about calves and ewe lambs and baby chicks? The place seems full of new little things lately."

"And kittens," added Alyssa. "The momma cat has her paws full with those."

And it was done. The dinner talk turned to the wonders of spring on a farm, the plants growing heavy, the smell of things alive everywhere.

Jake and Alyssa, each in a different way, kept the pirates, the intrigue, the castle and the worries alive even as they added to the talk at dinner. And not too many days after that, Jake, Alyssa, and Eugenie found themselves hearing too much about these subjects as the whole kingdom began to shiver as if it had caught a cold.

In the castle, the King and Queen fretted and paced. She went one way, he went the other. Both stopped at a window and then paced back toward each other like caged creatures. The kingdom, so peaceful, so complete just one year ago, a kingdom that one neighboring king called it the "Charmed Kingdom," was beginning to feel what the King called the collywobbles. He told his wife that he got up every day feeling as if he had eaten something that didn't agree with him. His stomach swooped and swirled with uneasiness. He thought he saw faces peering out from the hiding places where the castle walls crossed in complicated stone work. There were natural hiding places in the shadows there, and the King had been raised in this castle and knew all the nooks and crannies. But now they seemed filled, he told his wife, with plotters and schemers and enemies posing as friends. And there been recent news of pirates making all this castle intrigue even worse.

The pirates were common on the coast, but almost never bothered anyone inland. It seemed they needed to stay on the coast so they could hastily retreat to their boats if the King's men attacked. But now, the reports said, now they were boldly coming inland, stealing sheep and even cattle. One report told of pirates taking boys from farms, boys just old enough to make sailors. The pirates, who had always escaped from armed men by running, now were said to ride horses, and ride them well. Some new kind of pirate was abroad in the land.

The King sighed. "If I lead the army against the pirates, the castle will be left unguarded and that unholy clan of Arbuckle Beauregard and his new wife's ambitious family will be into every kind of mischief."

His wife added, "They seem to be making deals with the other families. I only hear a few things. Everyone hushes up when I appear. But a few of my most loyal ladies tell me that they too get hushed whispers as soon as they enter a room. So it has become hard to tell exactly what is going on. But, dear, I think they might just be bored. My father always said that peace bored some kinds of people, and they just had to make trouble where there was none. He said that keeping them guessing was the best thing. Don't let the peace be peaceful, he was fond of saying."

The King reached his window and paced back toward his wife. "Your father was a wise man. But I am not sure what the ridiculous Beauregard family could really do. His new wife's family, on the other hand, had a number of known scoundrels and ne'er-do-wells. Even before they married, I warned that silly man that he would be marrying into malcontents and fools. They are largely aggressive and stupid—that most deadly of combinations that account for many of the world's ills."

They both paused as they met between the windows, and both sighed at the same time as if they were doing some dance steps decorated with a long and sorrowful sigh right in the middle of the dance. On the wall behind them was a magnificent tapestry that told the story of the early kingdom with cunning figures emerging from a forest carrying sharp sticks and followed by large wolves at their sides. Women and men both emerged and circled into larger and larger rings that finally formed the castle walls as people became stones, stones became walls, walls united to form the great castle. Flags of yellow and red, green and blue and rusty red and black—flags of the early great families—flew from the finished ramparts. The tapestry was decorated with blue and red birds carrying sticks in their beaks, and in the distance, tiny versions of these birds were making nests on the castle walls. The King and Queen stopped and turned to the tapestry as if they had never seen it before.

The King said, "There. That's what we serve. The past. Everything and everyone who came before us. Sometimes I wake up in the morning, and before I put a foot on the floor, I can feel the weight of them all. Like they are sitting on my chest, and I have to lift them to even get out of bed. 'The ghosts,' I call them. 'Get up and scatter the ghosts,' I say to myself."

"Dear, maybe everyone in the world feels that way sometimes. Everyone gets up and…"

"Of course. Of course. If I learned one thing from *my* father, it was that being a king should never be separated from being a person. Everybody is the king; the king is everybody. For the longest time I thought that was just something he said when he felt that being a king was difficult. But he meant, I learned, that it was something I should remind myself about every minute of the day."

"I was going to say, dear, before you interrupted, that everyone has to decide every day what he or she will do with that day. Will it be ghosts sitting on shoulders all day? Or will we take a deep breath and get on with making the future?"

"I apologize for the interruption. I will try to be a better listener." He put his arm around his wife's waist, and together they studied the ancient tapestry, its story, colors, meanings. "And also, dear," he continued, "I am not going to lead a hundred armed men across the country in the spring rains chasing tens of pirates stealing sheep. Twenty years ago, yes. Absolutely. But the charms of tent living have faded for me. And I sleep my best sleep next to you, of course."

The Queen smiled and leaned her head on his shoulder. "The boredom of peace is so wonderful. How can we teach the people to love the boredom of peace? Flowers, weddings, babies, dances, more babies, more flowers and then feasts and cousins and music. Yes, music! And more music." She laughed and pointed at the tapestry. "I hadn't noticed before. Do you see it? Right there. Behind the biggest wolf, but in the distance. It looks like a tiny house or something. What is that?" She moved closer, looked up at one corner. Then she got a small stool, climbed on top of it and peered hard at the threads' cleverness in making the picture. "Right there."

The King stood on tip toes and squinted. "It looks like a small cottage just at the edge of the woods. I never saw it before. It's so small that it almost looks like a mistake the weavers made, maybe some extra thread just tucked in near the big tree."

The Queen studied the tiny house. "I don't know why it looks familiar. Have you ever seen one like it?"

"It's so small that it could be any cottage..."

"But those colors," she said. "Those colors aren't anywhere else on the tapestry. Maybe it was added later. This piece is nearly four hundred years old. It has been cleaned and someone might have added this little house. Now when I look at the whole picture, I see the little house clearly."

"Well," said the King. "At least there are no pirates anywhere in this picture. Maybe the pirates will just go away after they have enough sheep. No. I know they will become even bolder and come even farther inland if I do nothing. I would like to deceive myself. But I am too old to believe myself."

His wife went to get a taller stool so she could view the upper corner of the tapestry better still. Now she had her nose very close to the fabric as if she were going to sniff it. Or take a bite.

The King stood behind her in case she wobbled off the stool. "You know, my dear, now we both have new worries."

"I think I know where I have seen this little house."

"Everywhere?"

"No. *This* little house is not everywhere, not these colors, this door."

"Door? How can you even see a door in that little splotch

of threads? There is no door, certainly not windows."

"Oh yes. Look very closely and you can see the thread changes colors to make the windows. This was woven so that you would have to come this close to see how everything is there: door, windows, the little roof slope."

The Queen came down from her perch, the King paced back to the far window, and both took up their worries again. The King paused at his window, "We will take this Beauregard nonsense up with the Council."

The Queen cautioned, "Just be careful about who on the Council might benefit from allegiance to those silly people. Who might be bored with the peace of their lives."

"Thank you, dear," said the King. "That is wise caution."

The Queen looked at him as if he might not be taking her seriously, but she decided he was truly worried — about many things: the pirates, the Beauregard family, and he had recently mentioned that after eating, he didn't feel comfortable for hours. She had suggested that he eat less and see if that helped. But he had insisted that eating too much was not the problem. He felt, he said, as if the joy had gone out of eating altogether. She put her hand on his shoulder, and they looked at the tapestry together. She wondered why she had not seen the tiny cottage before now. And she sighed.

Michael Strelow

Chapter 8

The King and Queen posed in front of the complicated and beautiful tapestry that told and retold the story of their people. The Beauregard family had recently declared that Arbuckle Beauregard III, who had recently married their daughter, was the real and rightful king. Arbuckle still basked in the glow of the false belief among the people at court that he had somehow been responsible for the miracle at the end of his wedding. The flowers on all the tables where hundreds of farmers and their wives and children were eating, those flowers that Arbuckle himself had taken from all their gardens to decorate his wedding, those beautiful flowers had turned into coins and rained onto the tables, astounding everyone, royal or common. In an instant Arbuckle hid his surprise and so it was assumed that somehow he had made the miracle happen. The farmers took home the money for their flowers, Arbuckle was elevated into a kind of magician, and he never said one word to deny it. The deed was done. The magic was accounted for. The Beauregard family was returned to the high esteem it had two hundred years ago when Thomas Beauregard had won the battle that settled the kingdom and ended forty years of civil war.

The slow descent of the family from Thomas down to Arbuckle took those two hundred years, years that seem long to us but are actually the blink of an eye in the world of those history keepers who carefully record the families and their political gifts. And now the alliance—the *deal* is maybe a better way of thinking about it—between Eugenie the princess, Alyssa the farm girl, Jake and Arbuckle, well, this deal began to seem fragile from any way you looked at it. Each one knew about the girls having changed places. Each one found an advantage to the switch. Or they had, anyway. The deal was wearing as thin as the knees on a gardener's pants. The princess become farm girl, the farm girl now roaming the palace as royalty, Arbuckle the silly fop become important statesman, and Jake who had recently roamed the treetops with a beautiful furry tail, all felt how fragile and doomed the deal had become.

Outside the castle, that old joker, spring, with its summer-like days that could be followed by a blowing day left over from winter, that faker and pretender, swirled up and down the ancient castle walls and must have smiled at how the castle folk now scurried around and furrowed their brows. Nothing lasts very long, spring might have whispered to them. Just wait. All will change. And it did.

Arbuckle Beauregard The Third had married into an old family that had fallen on difficult financial times. Their ancient name, one that had roots in the oldest words used to describe the actual dirt of the farms, once again rang through the land as they linked their fortunes to Arbuckle, his heroic saving of the kingdom, and then his new title of Water Master, Earl of the Springs. Dirt and water joined in marriage; all they needed to be complete was the sun itself.

Arbuckle had married a Soyle-Regolith, and she proudly carried her people's claim to be older and more substantial than any other family in the kingdom. They argued that all other families, all other names, all other bloodlines were really just Johnny-come-latelys. And further, they argued, they were the originals, the first, the earth-givers themselves. Dear Anna Soyle-Regolith, Arbuckle's wife, knew the stories, of course. Her family educated her. But she had no ambition to overturn the kingdom, to restore her family, to set the crooked straight. She believed she was raising up her family's fortunes by connecting with the Beauregards, and that was enough. But her father and mother saw the marriage as only the first step in returning the kingdom to its rightful rulers. They believed that all would be possible now that the family suddenly had money and newly glowed in the eyes of the King's court. After the wedding they breathed a sigh of relief that the deed was done. They even accepted that the flowers turning into money was probably the doing of Arbuckle, and all credit should be due his family. But, of course, now they would add his family to their claim.

Arbuckle himself, though he knew better, began to believe that he was responsible for the two acts of magic: hadn't he saved the kingdom from its own bad water (the girls helped, of course, but still), and hadn't the coins rained down from the flowers at the wedding just as he stood to give a toast? Coincidence? He thought that one coincidence, yes. But two coincidences? Certainly there was magic afoot.

The Princess Eugenie saw the whole thing coming like a rock rolling downhill getting bigger and bigger every second. Arbuckle knew she had changed places with the real princess who was now enjoying her garden on the farm and her brother, Jake. Jake knew too, of course, and seemed to be enjoying the whole new arrangement. And Princess Eugenie, formerly a farm girl longing for the advantages of the castle, was also enjoying her world. That made three "enjoyings" and just one Arbuckle, whatever he was thinking. And then, of course, there was the Soyle-Regolith family whose frowns had recently been turned upside down.

Arbuckle had the key. If anyone were to find out that Princess Eugenie was really a farm girl with grand educational ambitions, the royal family might just come tumbling down. And so Arbuckle knew if he kept his secret, that Eugenie owed him a great debt. And if he told his secret—to his new in-laws—then *they* would be in his debt and have a direct claim on the throne. All Arbuckle could do each day was walk around smiling, smirking really, at his perfect power.

Let's see, he thought. Should I become a powerful figure in the kingdom this way? Or that way? Should I make it rain gold for myself this way? Or that way? And so, while the King and Queen fretted about the most recent attack of the sheep-stealing pirates and while the Soyle-Regolith family silently plotted to take over the kingdom, Arbuckle put on his newest green vest decorated with all the signs and insignias of his office as Grand Water Master (he had recently added "Grand" to his title to see if anyone noticed—they didn't). And then he walked abroad in the castle, smirking and nodding, nodding and smirking to all he passed by.

In his mind he heard them all thinking: "What a grand figure the new Grand Water Master cuts. He is a most fortunate man with his new wife and powerful position. Surely he has been favored by all manner of gods to be so fortunate. Oh lucky man! Oh favored one!" What they were really thinking was something very different, but what counted for him was the whirl and glow of words in his own mind.

Eventually, since it was a beautiful day, he wandered from the castle in his Water Master role checking water, mastering the countryside. He had a fine horse, a fine day and fine fettle—an unbeatable combination. As he rode he came to a great wood where many little streams were born. He had no desire to go into the woods since he would have to walk his horse or be lashed by low-hanging branches. Perched here on top of his horse, he was master of everything. He peered down a winding path going into the dark of the forest, and he thought, no. Not today. He should, though, in the future, send some men there to make certain the water sources were clean and pure. He made a note. He underlined the note. He put away his notebook and took a deep breath. Life was on the edge of unbearably delightful. Smirk gone, Arbuckle broke into a glorious smile.

At the edge of the forest more than one squirrel eyed this strange figure and his beautiful horse. But only one of the squirrels was Jake who paused for a second, though he had just heard the whistle. He should return immediately to the old couple, but he wanted to stay a moment longer high in the tree just where the sun swept into the leaves on this afternoon. Jake heard the whistle again, this time longer and louder, and so he sniffed twice and scampered into the forest to return to being a farm boy again.

Arbuckle heard no whistle. But his horse did and pranced in a quick circle, his hooves making a pirouette like a two dancers joined at the hip. Two quick circles then stop. Arbuckle's eyes opened wide at having found himself suddenly part of the dance. He looked around for a snake. Sometimes a horse will dance if a snake crawls by. But there was no snake, just the afternoon wind tickling the new leaves and the warm sun on his regal green vest. He briefly thought he might ride into the forest and took a moment to peer down the path. Very quickly the path faded into the forest, the light seemed to dwindle there, and the sun that felt so fine on his official vest didn't do its duty in the shade of the woods.

And so Arbuckle thought he might take the long way back to the castle. The idea of having to spend any part of this fine afternoon with his wife's people or the scheming relatives on either side seemed unpleasant—the exact opposite of a beautiful day, a fine horse and a light breeze. He walked his horse vaguely in the direction of the castle, but he knew of a spring a few miles away that he hadn't inspected in a long time. Duty called. He smiled to himself and patted his horse affectionately on the neck. The beautiful beast craned his neck around to look at the rider, and his great brown eyes seemed to ask, "Where to?"

The spring, though not far away, was hidden by a long and graceful hill and a grove of trees, dense in the middle, and then ringed by young willows. There was shade, the gentle sound of water and the unspoken invitation to come and relax here. The water ran from the hillside not very far over the grass before it went underground and disappeared. And because there was no lake or even a small pond, there were no paths to the place, no trails where shepherds had led their flocks to drink, just the talking water and willows waving wispy branches with lime green young leaves in the sun.

There was always a sigh just about to come out of Arbuckle. But here, in this place, life was simple and good — no pretending to be what he wasn't, no one to answer to. Those two girls had lifted him out of his silliness and made him a better person. Those two girls... And now, alas, his wife's family was setting him against the King and Queen in ways that made him feel like he had a stomachache all the time. He knew it was not good when you had a stomachache all the time. That was the sign, he had learned, that he was being made to do something against his own better sense. That feeling in his stomach, how true it was. The spring water was saying many things — almost. He listened to the voices there and the almost-words that leaked out of the sound of the talking water. If only they would speak up. Just a little. He would be able to hear what they had to say and, he was certain, they would tell him what to do. He *knew* already what to do about protecting the water. The girls, Alyssa and Eugenie, had taught him that, and then they let him take the credit for saving the people of the kingdom. They had switched lives and giving him credit for their hard work was a small price to pay for their happiness.

And then Arbuckle did sigh, a sigh so loud and long that his horse lifted his head from where he had been eating the sweet, young grass that grew around the spring. Arbuckle's sigh seemed to hang in the air as if his very soul had come out of his mouth to have a look at the sunshine and spring, to get out of the dark and dizzy place inside him where confusion was the king.

Kings, queens, family crests and swords and shields and rampant golden animals prancing across heraldic colors all ran round his head like a tangled circus where all the acts were on at once. At his feet the spring was strong and talkative. Over his head the air smelled of the love of the land. Arbuckle sat.

There was no rock or log, so he sat down in the moist grass as if his legs would hold him up no longer. His wife's family wanted and wanted and wanted. He had known about their ambitions, how they felt they had been wronged by the King's family and how, now, they felt it should be they who sit on the throne and direct the Council and make the laws. But Anna had been sweet to him. And she was such good company. And his own family had said it was time for him to get married. Anna's family joining his would delight everyone in the kingdom and all would be well. And that's how easy it had been to get married and have a great feast and have all the flowers turn to money. But then, slowly at first, his wife's family had brought up the injustice they were suffering from, the unfairness of fate that might yet someday be corrected if only... And then they changed the subject. But soon, there it was again hanging in the air in every conversation: the rightful heirs to the kingdom, only getting what was their due, righting the wrongs of recent history.

And there were ancient uncles and aunts perched on chairs like fierce birds around the family room, each one seeming to have some beak-sharp thing to say about the King and Queen. Anna's mother and father then taking up the drumbeat with their own plans to wait for the day to set things right. As they should be! As they always should have been! How putting the world into proper alignment might make the crops grow better, the sun shine brighter, and the enemies of the kingdom fear and respect them even more. The pirates would be vanquished and driven back to sea. The rain storms would grow gentle and nourishing. And on… and on… and on.

Arbuckle Beauregard III began to feel the wet grass through his pants. The spring was no closer to telling him what to do. His horse swung his great and beautiful head around as if to ask Arbuckle an important question. The world waited, and he rose, brushed off his wet bottom and made his weary way to the side of his horse. He leaned on the huge warm flank, forehead and nose against quivering muscle. The horse's tail came around and flicked the back of Arbuckle's head. He wished he could sink into the horse right then and never come out, worry only about the next grass, where to put his great feet.

After a time with the spring having moved on now from words to song, the wind rising slightly, the horse impatient to move, Arbuckle mounted and began his way back to the castle and all the clatter and jangle there. He pulled his vest straight, adjusted his hat, clucked, "hup, hup" to his horse, and disappeared down the tiny path onto the great road toward his life.

Chapter 9

Both Alyssa and Eugenie, each bearing the other one's life and family, knew that Jake's birthday was coming soon. And though everyone loves their own birthday, Jake was even a greater lover of his. His eyes would begin to get brighter a week before and would remain glowing for a week after. The girls had begun to refer to this glow as "the birthday weeks." And Jake could be talked into staying on the ground for long periods of time during his birthday weeks. He would do chores with a whistle. He would "carry heavy loads with a light step," their father added with a smile. Birthdays just seemed to be a brilliant time for Jake. Oh, other people's birthdays were fine: the sweets, the flowers, the presents. But Jake thought that nothing finer in the world could sweep around each year than the celebration of your own arrival in this world of trees and secret sisters and, now, the chance to play squirrel.

He had been visiting the old couple's garden and somehow they both had known that his birthday was coming up. Maybe it was the glow, who knows? But the old lady presented Jake with a small gift wrapped in brown paper and tied with a red ribbon.

She explained, "This is not a usual gift. This is a gift for you to give away to someone else." Jake looked puzzled and took another bite of his cookie. She continued, "You may choose to whom. I think you will know, but anyone you choose is the right person. The gift is for you to give as a gift. That's the important part."

"But if I want, I can keep it?"

"Oh no. The gift is much better if you, for your own birthday, give it to someone else. It's like lifting the corner of the world and finding a new world there. Some people call it 'turning the tables.' But, no matter. When you do give it, I want you to think very hard how it feels to be giving a gift on your own birthday. And remember that. Be sure to concentrate on how that feels. You will like what you find, I think."

The old man laughed. "Pretty spooky stuff, isn't it, Jake? She has her ways. Her ways." He laughed again and then fell silent.

"I understand," Jake said quietly. The people who could turn him into a squirrel and let him run the treetops, well, they could teach him a new way to go about birthdays too. The package felt soft and warm like something made of fine cloth but alive. He squeezed it gently and looked at the old woman to see if that was allowed.

"You won't hurt it by squeezing. But be careful not to tear the paper, though. Open it carefully when you get home so it doesn't spill. Then decide who to give it to. Oh, and it belongs with its like kind."

Jake wrinkled his nose. "Like kind?"

"You'll see. That will make sense when you see it. It's an early present so that it doesn't get mixed up with your other celebrations. I know that turning nine has great pith and moment." She laughed and patted Jake's head. "Pith and moment, that means that a ninth birthday is fabulous. It's the last birthday with only one number. After that, it will be two numbers for a long, long time. Enjoy it. You will be a fine nine-year-old."

He was due home soon, but paused long enough for a birthday hug from each of them before making his way out of the garden and down the path home. The package felt even warmer, maybe because he had been holding it against himself. He began to whistle and think of a song to sing. His feet felt birthday-light on the path, his shoes feathered. He considered the treetops, how he might get home from one to the other but decided the sunny path was just fine for now.

Soon the barn came into view, and Alyssa in her garden was resting on her hoe and seemed lost in thought. Jake quickly put the gift behind his back and waved at her while heading for the house. He wanted to open it in private. It was the first gift he had ever received that he had to give away. Up the stairs two at a time, into his attic space where the roof came sloping down to meet the floor, and then pulled the red ribbon to open it.

Inside was dirt. It was very nice dirt, but it was dirt. Jake laughed. It must be some kind of old person joke. Ninth-birthday dirt! The old couple must be laughing now, poking each other at the fine joke they played. Jake looked closely. Maybe there was something hidden in the dirt: a jewel, a magic talisman. With one finger he pushed the dirt around on the wrapping until there was only a thin layer covering the paper. No anything. Dirt.

Jake took a deep breath and began to think about the second part of the gift. He had to give it to someone else, and he would know who that person was. The gift would be perfect for that person. Very quickly he thought of Alyssa, his mad gardener sister, who as soon as she finished her chores could always be found tinkering with her garden. She trimmed and poked and mumbled to the young plants. She talked about the young vegetables as if they were her dolls (which now she never played with) at a tea party. She would say to them, "See how big you have grown." And she would show him the squash babies with the flowers still clinging to them. And he would always pretend to be very impressed with these babies because she was a good sister. A good gardener. Father was always trying to interest Jake in how the wheat grew, how the animals became healthy and fat. But he talked about it differently than did Alyssa. She always spoke in a kind of hushed voice as if someone were listening close by who shouldn't be hearing her secrets.

Alyssa! The dirt must be given to Alyssa.

Jake rewrapped the dirt being careful not to spill one crumb. He fastened it all up again with the red bow. He would give it to her now, though his birthday was not today.

He found her, of course, in her garden.

"Alyssa, because my birthday is coming up soon, I want to give *you* a present. I think it will be fun to give presents to other people for my birthday week." He held out the package to her while she was kneeling and pulling weeds. She smiled at him.

"Jake, you are my strange and wonderful brother. What a good idea giving presents to other people for your birthday. However did you think...? Never mind. I accept this gift. And I congratulate you on your invention—the birthday ungift. Should we call it that?" All the time she spoke she was unwrapping the present, carefully folding the red ribbon and tucking it in her pocket. She opened the paper and opened her eyes and mouth wide in surprise. "Yeah. Good choice for any gardener. Jake, you are the best brother in the world."

Jake couldn't tell if she was pretending or what. She seemed to be genuinely pleased with the gift of dirt. But she was a good pretender too. She could be fooling him. She had many ways to fool with him.

She smelled the dirt with a great, slow sniff. "This dirt has fine promise, Jake," she declared. "It's beautiful and dark and loamy." She took the package carefully and began to sprinkle it on her garden. "My favorites will get it first," she whispered as if she didn't want the other plants to hear. "Then these over here just because they are a little spindly. Maybe not enough sun. And over here the flowers should get a little too because, well, they *are* flowers, after all. And flowers deserve more. That's what they think, anyway. Just look at them. They think they deserve the best and the most. But they probably do, and so a little more birthday dirt over here, and over here."

Jake studied his sister. She was having a grand time clucking to her plants and making the dirt come out even over the whole garden. With a final shake she emptied the paper and folded it neatly and put it in her pocket.

"There," she said. And she clapped her hands together to free the final grains of dirt, and they drifted down on her garden. "All done. I thank you, Jake. My garden thanks you. And the flowers thank you even more profusely than the vegetables. They are just like that, you know. They have to do everything better than everyone else. And you can't eat most of them. Except the nasturtiums; they are very delicious in salads. And some of them can taste quite peppery. Only Mother and I eat them in salads now, but maybe you and Father can be convinced to join us."

Jake thought that all this felt so right that the old couple must have meant for the dirt to go to Alyssa all along. And the next day he was sure of it.

Alyssa was shaking him awake. "Jake, Jake. Where did you get that dirt? Come and look." Slowly Jake stirred himself trying to understand what she was on about while the fog of sleep lifted.

"What? What are you talking about?"

"The dirt. Where did you get the dirt from? Look!"

Jake looked out the window and didn't see what she was talking about. At first. She said, "My garden. Look at my garden."

Jake narrowed his eyes and peered at her garden. Past the barn, the garden glowed with green newness. But it always did that. What? He thought.

"See how much bigger everything is? That happened over night. That cannot happen unless..." She sat on his bed. "Oh," she said. "I see."

She patted his head as she always did. "You visited the old couple, didn't you? And they gave you this dirt for me. And they wrapped it up..."

"Not exactly," Jake interrupted. "They didn't give me the dirt and tell me to give it to you. Exactly. Not exactly."

"What then?"

"I got the dirt as a birthday present but only if I gave it *to* someone. A birthday present that I had to give away. I know. It was a funny idea. But they are funny people."

The dirt had been a magic gift, he guessed. Alyssa's garden was growing like their garden—ahead of everyone, ahead of the rest of springtime! The dirt was as if summer itself had been wrapped in the paper with the red ribbon.

Alyssa sat and looked out Jake's window. "Jake. Let's keep this gift just between you and me."

"And the Truebloods, too," Jake said, using their name to see if Alyssa knew it too.

"Yes, of course. Them too. But the gift of special dirt. That's just between us, agreed? I'm not sure I want to try to explain all this to Mother and Father. To *anyone*. I will claim that the difference in my garden came from my special fertilizer tea. I got that recipe from them too, you know."

Jake was fully awake now. "I know. And..." He paused and looked his sister in the eye. "And you know that I know, well, everything." He thought it would be a good time to get this all straight.

"You knew all along. Eugenie—okay, Alyssa—and I realized that you and Arbuckle knew we had switched places and by some miracle no one else saw it."

Jake said, "I kept your secret. Can you keep a secret, too?"

"Of course, Jake. I am a princess living the life I really wanted, a gardener. Keeping one more secret will not be a problem. Secrets are hanging all over my life—every time I talk to our parents, every time I go to school, every day, every minute I get to spend in my garden. I love my secrets."

Jake took a deep breath. And then in one long rush, like letting out a colt that had been too long cooped up in the barn, his full story came galloping out, and Alyssa's mouth dropped open. Her eyes grew wide. He told of going back after the first time being a squirrel, how they all went together into the darkest part of the woods, the sounds, the silence, the branches, the thrill of being loose again in the treetops.

When he had finished, she said, "A squirrel? Of all the choices? A squirrel? Well, I guess that makes sense for you. When you told me before, I believed you but thought they only made it *seem* like you were a squirrel. Now I see, though. You really were a squirrel!"

"I could be anything. But a squirrel seemed to me the most interesting thing to be. Would you be a worm? In your garden? A worm, or a pill bug or a snake maybe. How about a snake? Every fall a new skin. Or a…"

"I see. And, no, not a snake. Definitely not a snake. Maybe a butterfly. Or a bird. A bird, yes."

"I'll see if they will let you be a bird. But they told me it was only for me."

"No, Jake. It is a gift for you. I love the dirt gift. You keep the squirrel thing to yourself. Your secret is safe with me."

Chapter 10

But the secret could not stay with Alyssa, it turned out. Eugenie had to know too. The world of the castle was slowly turning upside down. What everyone knew was true was suddenly not true. Or so it seemed. The King and Queen, it was reported, were scrambling to keep order. And the order they were trying to keep was their family on top, the old order.

And then there were the pirates, who were usually only a small problem in this kingdom because pirates stayed on the ocean, and most of the kingdom was inland, except for the coast where cliffs and small, stony beaches protected that land. But recently, pirates were being starved on their boats and the small islands where they usually raided for food had all been swept clean by great hurricanes, it was said, and that left the natives working to gather what food they could. And the pirates were left to scramble for themselves.

So, two kinds of scrambling: King and Queen, pirates. And the old rules or at least the old ways of doing things went out the window. New ways, no rules—that would be how the kingdom lived from now on. The new wife, Anna Soyle-Regolith, of Arbuckle Beauregard III found herself clinging to the simple, old ways in which she was NOT Queen, Arbuckle was NOT in charge of anything but keeping the water pure, and there were parties and balls and festive ceremonies that everyone would agree were delightful and stimulating and would provide days of delicious conversation afterwards.

But the whole society of the castle began to wobble like a tree with rotten roots flailing in the wind. There were signs at first. The King sent out a few men to chase away the pirates. The men had not been heard from in more than a month. The Soyle-Regolith family began to keep to themselves and invite into their circle only the royalty in the castle who they thought they could convince that the King and Queen were not the rightful rulers.

"Some people grow fat on war," announced the King's chief councilor, Old Garibald. He was old but spry. After pronouncing this he popped up from his chair and began to pace around the chamber like he might be looking for something he lost on the floor. The other members looked down at the table in front of them and waited.

"Those are the ones making messes now. They want to tip over the cart and see what falls out for them. They don't care who is under the cart, what happens to the poor horse, where the beets roll to, who gets crushed. They just stand there glaring at that cart and itching to turn it over because they cannot stand things the way they are." Old Garibald sawed the air with one arm, the other hand shoved deep into the huge pocket in his velvet vest. A gold chain around his neck wagged with each word and clinked against the medallion of office pinned to his vest. Saw, wag, clink. Saw, wag, clink. Old Garibald painted pictures with words for the assembled Council: the kingdom was at great risk from within; the kingdom was at great risk from without. Pirates in ever greater numbers snatched bleating lambs from farmers' fields, and sedition—that invitation to riot and attack authority—was creeping from room to room in the castle.

Old Garibald stopped and looked from councilor to councilor as if to accuse each one of being part of that creeping insurrection; each person held his gaze to profess innocence. One councilor even older than Old Garibald, whose name was Glen Glenn, looked at his fingers as if counting them. Old Garibald paused his glance long on

Glenn and then decided that counting your fingers was the most likely explanation for Glenn looking away. He was not capable of sedition, probably would get the wrong number of fingers, too.

And so the meeting began and continued this way and so did the next and the next. Some version of this uneasiness, some version of Old Garibald's pacing by one member or another, some version of the creeping feeling that all was not right and getting worse and the only thing left was the waiting—all this began to seep among the walls of the castle as if it had crept out of the Council room and flowed down the ancient castle hallways.

Jake was going to be nine years old, his birthday falling unfortunately right in the middle of this new uneasiness. But a birthday is still a birthday. Jake was already delighted with the kind of gift he had received that he had to give away in order for it to become a gift. At first he could not see what Alyssa was looking at in her garden. The first day after the gift of dirt had been spread among the plants, the garden looked the same to him. But the second day! Then he could clearly see the big change. And so could his father and mother. They each asked Alyssa what had happened to her garden, and she patiently explained that she had been cooking up this new fertilizer that you could spread like tea, and the plants seemed to brighten up and grow fiercely. She didn't think the magic dirt gift would be useful to explain just now. She would let Jake have his joyful present. And she *had* been brewing a kind of brown soup that the old woman had taught her, brewed out of certain forest roots and then scraps and leaves and twigs and even the scum off the top of the pond water. And after many days the brown tea was ready. It was good fertilizer but nothing like the dirt that had been wrapped with a red ribbon that she now kept in her drawer in her bedroom. Whatever was happening in the garden, she would laugh and tell her parents that the tea was at work there.

Father was very interested in the tea but thought that he would not be able to make enough quantities or fast enough for his fields, and so he would continue to spread manure. But Alyssa's garden, Jake noticed, was quickly catching up to the old couple's garden as if the soil from there had brought all its magic along with the small handful in the gift. Jake had also been given the gift of being a squirrel, had let the old man build a house of branches around him, had scampered through the tops of the great linden tree the old people called a lime tree. So powerful garden soil, magic dirt—who knew, changing the sky to pink? Everything was possible, and, in addition, his ninth birthday sat right there soon. The world was fine and exciting. No pirates, no whispered plots here.

Jake went about his chores in the barn.

It was not long before, it seemed to Jake, that all the things that *could* happen, did.

"Psst, Jake. Meet at the old couple's garden when you're done with your chores." The voice seemed to come from the ceiling of the barn where mice and owls and spiders and cats all came together with the eyes of sunlight at the edges of the dark where a shingle was broken, a hole bored by a flicker. The voice was familiar, but it was the other one, the one he didn't hear every day. The other Alyssa. The original sister. That one. "Don't let anyone see you go. You know how." And the voice echoed for a second and was gone.

By the time Jake reached the edge of the garden, he could see the girls—both sisters—sitting on the stone bench talking at the same time. He watched for a second before revealing himself. He had come by tree, some low branches, some higher, but all the way by tree until the edge of the clearing that opened on the old couple's garden. He couldn't hear the girls yet but he could see them talking excitedly as if they were in a hurry to fill each other up with news.

They saw him, waved, kept talking, and he made his way through the beginnings of the zinnias to the marigolds to the pea vines to the young squash plants stretching out over the dark soil.

"Jake, sit. We both have something you have to hear." Which one? Both of them, but just the one. It was Alyssa in both cases, but Jake could see that the Alyssa who spoke was wearing finely stitched clothes while the other wore homespun cloth stitched in the village way. He knew which was which. The girls looked at each other. "You first, no you first," they both said. Jake thought the whole business was getting funnier by the second: two Alyssas, two talking at once, two looking at each other as if in a mirror. It seemed to Jake that maybe some kind of show was taking place, like when the traveling troupe came through the village and barked out their silly plays in front of a purple curtain. Only here, the old couple's garden was applauding in its colorful way, the girls acting out an impossible tale, the sun lighting up everything.

"Jake! Jake, pay attention. This is important."

"Yes, Jake. Listen carefully. A lot depends on this. We have news. Not very good news."

Jake looked back and forth between them nodding to assure them he was listening, but he really wasn't. Not very well. The whole thing was funny and very strange at the same time. He remembered when he had shocked his real sister by recognizing her from behind as she milked a cow. It was easy for him. But now his mind wandered instead of paying attention. Anyway, it was his birthday week, and they both had to be nice to him.

One of the Alyssas took his face gently in her two hands and turned his head toward them. "Now, Jake. What we are going to tell you is very secret." She let go of his face. "Very secret. No one can know this, not Mother or Father. Not yet. It would give us away. *Especially* not Mother and Father. Do you understand?"

Jake thought of one of his father's horses, the one always on the left when pulling as a team, the one his father had told him had to be told clearly what to do while the other one always seemed to know exactly what to do. Jake always liked that horse best because, like him, it seemed to always be listening to some other voices, and you had to get its attention.

Again a sisterly voice, this time close to his ear. "There could be great danger, Jake. For you. For all of us. The pirates that used to be just on the coast, well, it seems they are everywhere now. They were reported a few miles from the village. Only two or maybe three of them, but just the same. There they were stealing sheep."

"And one horse, the farmer said. Pirates on horses! Not good. Not good at all."

The two Alyssas, one on each side, stared at him until they were sure they had his attention. Then one began again. "Pirates here near the village. No one could remember that happening before. They were always a problem, but a far-away problem."

"But they are only half the problem, Jake. The second part is not bad yet, but could get very bad soon. You remember Arbuckle? Of course, you do. Well, his wife's family is cooking up something unpleasant for the kingdom. They want to take over. To take over everything, everywhere. And throw out the King and Queen..."

"My father and mother..."

"… and put people in jail who don't agree with them until they have the Council in their greedy pocket. There will be a mess, and I think soon. The King and Queen, of course, will not give up their rule easily. Not to people like the Soyle-Regolith family."

"My father and mother, it seems — Eugenie has made this very clear — will use the army, but the army has been…"

"Bought!"

"Yes, bought. Or at least money is everywhere filling pockets with promises of more money. And the army is doing what it should. So far. But no one trusts…"

"Anything. Anymore."

Jake felt as if he were in a tree top in a wind storm. It blew this way. It blew that. He swayed down and then swayed up. The girls swirled and blew and finished each other's sentences. The whole kingdom and all the stories of all the old names and shields and crests — all these swirled too. All that clear history now was being tossed and hurled about by the girls' words. Things were becoming unhinged like the time the heavy barn door had sagged and then had fallen, tearing a part of the support post with it. The door was coming off. The big beams of the world suddenly creaking and groaning.

Jake listened as the girls made the picture clearer and clearer. Pirates and what they called sedition that he understood to be the wheels coming off the cart of the kingdom. He felt that if he could just be freed by his sisters, free to swing up into a tree and find his way to the top branches where the tree was youngest in twig and leaf and he was lightest and the world was fine and all the way down there below him…

When they finished, Jake had been conscripted, that's what they both said. Conscripted meant joined up, they told him. He had been conscripted into the fight. And the pirates met the castle disaster when the King was forced to lead a troop of soldiers into the countryside leaving the castle guards untended. The Queen was captured, sort of. She was confined to her rooms in comfort. They told her she would be treated well, like an important family member. But no longer the queen. She had no choice but to retire while Eugenie escaped in her gardening clothes.

And here they were. The old couple was nowhere to be seen. Nothing stirred in the house. Even the cat was missing. The girls looked around the garden as if pirates might come swooping down at any minute, scoop them all up and take them to sea.

Without sighing out loud, Jake sighed—all inside. It was his birthday week. There were pirates about. Soldiers about. People taking sides. The Queen locked up. And his mother and father were going about the farm business just as if all the skies were sunny, all the pieces in the right places, all the stars in the night sky lined up properly. But Jake could feel the darkness coming.

Chapter 11

The pirate part came first. The pirates had learned to set a fire, and while the farmers were fighting the fire, they would steal animals: chickens, ducks and geese too and anything not firmly fixed to the earth. They had wagons now and hid them in the trees until the fire was burning well. Then the looting began while one of them came to help the farmers fight the fire but actually was there keeping track of all the men while his friends stole everything. The spring grass was barely dry and difficult to start. But once the heat dried some of the grass, even the greenest blades would flare up and burn.

One of the King's most trusted councilors supposed that if a person thought about the pirates coming inland just as the Soyle-Regolith family began their challenge to the King and Queen, then one might consider the two things connected. The councilor, who always wore a vest of red—in fact never called it a red vest, always a vest of red—tucked his thumbs into the small pockets on each side of the vest, harrumphed (twice) and began to explain to the King just how the Soyle-Regolith plotters might connect with the pirates. The King, not wanting to spend each day fending off the plotters, suggested that the pirates might just be looking for food.

"Bah," said the councilor. "Bah, and bah. I once heard a man say that sometimes evidence was more convincing than other times, such as a trout in the milk."

"Well, we must be vigilant then," said the King.

The Councilor, who was too old and too well trusted to be worried about offending the King, repeated his bah several more times while he gathered his thoughts. "And further even than bah, there is an unhealthy collusion afoot. A remarkable humbug in the wind. An ill wind blowing from both of them together."

While the King and the councilor debated the exact connections between pirates and a historical and noble family of the realm, Arbuckle and his somewhat new wife also debated.

"I think," said she, "that my mother is growing old and sees her chance."

Arbuckle, who hated talking about this business altogether, was daydreaming of his afternoon by the spring, his beautiful horse grazing nearby, the sun on his shoulders. But not for long. "Yes, of course," he said. His wife had tugged at his sleeve to get his attention. She found herself often these days having to return Arbuckle's attention to matters at hand. Sometimes just a touch or a tug would do it.

She said, "And Father thinks there is nothing to lose, after all. What could the King do? Throw us all in jail? There are far too many of us, Father maintains. With far too many friends at court and in the army. Father says," and Anna lowered her voice and posed with hands on hips: "'The test will come. Right will win out. It always does. It often just takes its own sweet time doing it.'"

Arbuckle sighed. He found himself sighing very often these confusing days. And a sigh often felt good, as if he were expelling the whole tiresome business out of his lungs to be blown away by the slightest breeze. He longed for the days when he had been a hero to the entire kingdom. He had heard huzzahs and trumpets in his name. There was a procession in which he had been named the Water Master for the kingdom for his part in discovering and curing the great water sickness. He, Arbuckle Beauregard The Third, had made the actual announcement, had convened the councilors, prodded the King, made the history out of what the girls had provided. Those days, ah, those days, he thought. What color and pageantry! And then they had paid the greatest artist in the land to paint his picture to be hung on the wall with his ancestors. His painting was a tiny bit bigger; he had seen to that. The artist thought it wouldn't matter if he made the canvas just this much bigger, and he held up his fingers a smidgeon apart.

His wife, Arbuckle, the King and his councilor, and then Alyssa and Eugenie—pairs all thinking about the same thing in different ways.

Alyssa and Eugenie, having saved the kingdom before, were making plans. The others were creasing their brows and fretting, and while creasing brows and tsking *were* doing something, the girls were laying out their shoulds and ought tos in order to keep the kingdom safe.

The girls had already discussed power: what it was, who had it, how it could be useful. There was the King, of course, and his army, so far very loyal. Then there was the ancient Soyle-Regolith family and all the clouds of historical glory they claimed. And then there were the pirates.

Eugenie claimed the pirates were a problem because no one knew exactly who they were. They only had a name, nothing else. Everyone knew what a pirate was but no one knew *who* a pirate was. Alyssa wrote that down. The old couple's garden cupped them like a friendly hand.

Alyssa put down her notes. "We don't know how many or who, is that right?"

"We only know what; that's right." The girls looked at each other as they often did, cocked their heads together, laughed a little at their greatly similar faces that clothing had disguised for all this time. "Jake. What do you know about pirates?"

Jake heard but was pretending he didn't. Somehow

being almost nine was not actually being nine. When he was nine, he thought, he would be much more like an adult. He would think thoughts like his mother and father did; he would give people advice. He would shake hands like a man, laugh loudly, sneeze into a red handkerchief, lean against a fence post with one leg cocked and a wheat straw in his mouth.

"Jake?" Eugenie asked. "What have you heard about the pirates?"

Jake thought carefully and then decided he had a few more days to be eight and would not rush being nine. "They wear patches on one eye." He held up one finger to indicate that that would be the first thing he knew. "And the reason they do, is they keep one eye in the dark so when they go down inside the ship they can raise the patch and see in the dark better with the uncovered eye."

Jake waited for this to impress his sisters. This important information he had heard from a boy in school who had lived on a farm on the sea coast. The boy pronounced his information carefully and included lifting an invisible patch suddenly and being able to see in the dark of a ship. Jake thought it made perfect sense. If you closed your eyes for a minute before going into the dark barn, you could see much better. Fact. "And number two," Jake's second finger went up, "they sometimes eat children—girls mostly. But if they get very hungry they *will* eat a boy. A young one." The friend from the sea coast had been clear about this. Pirates mostly ate girls. And when one of the other boys had asked why, why mostly girls, the boy had thought a moment and then pronounced them more delicious. Jake remembered thinking this piece of information was not as good or as useful as the eye patch information. But considering the source, he was willing to include it in what he knew about pirates.

His sisters listened to him without rolling their eyes, but finally, Alyssa broke first and rolled hers. "Oh, Jake. I will accept the first one. Not the second."

Eugenie said, "Come over here. I am the princess and you have to do what I say." But her smile gave her away. She was his real sister and so had the right to rub his head with her knuckles—a little too hard always. And so Jake skittered off a ways and kept Alyssa, his newer, kinder sister, between him and Eugenie.

"You two have your talk. I have business way over here on the edge of the garden. Mrs. Trueblood asked me to check on... to check on those tomatoes. The stakes. I'll be doing that while you two talk." And he was off.

The girls returned to their plan that carefully considered power—who had it, what did it look like, what could they do about it. And, over all, how could they ask the old couple for their help. Once again.

The girls looked around to see if maybe the old couple had appeared in the garden, but they were nowhere to be seen. Jake pretended to fix the tomatoes at the far edge of the garden. The cottage looked empty, no smoke from the chimney, the red door closed tight, the window blank.

Princess Eugenie, the one presently living in the castle, spoke first. "We have, I think, a number of problems developing."

Alyssa thought that the princess language had taken hold in her friend, that now she really *sounded* like the princess she had become. It was a kind of seriousness in the voice, a tinkle like a tiny silver bell being rung far away that accompanied her voice whenever she spoke. Alyssa wondered if she had had that tinkle when she was the princess. Had she lost her tinkle?

Eugenie clearly set out the who-was-who part of the castle plotting. It was complicated with many plotters and some who just went along and then others who waited to see what would happen so they could congratulate the winners and join them. What surprised Alyssa was the old family names Eugenie mentioned that had been loyal to her father and mother but now were not necessarily loyal anymore. The Fildriges and the Comportenses and the Scatton-Bundys—she had played with their children, traveled to their country homes, ridden their horses. Now, alas, plotters or at least on the fence.

Eugenie continued, "And so time will tell who does what, I suppose."

"How much time? Is this all going to happen soon?"

"I have to admit, I can't tell," Eugenie said sadly, but with her voice tinkle still working. She sighed. They both sighed. The plan was not coming easily.

Alyssa thought in terms of a garden. Tend it, water it, hoe out the weeds, add fertilizer then stakes to hold up the weak stems. Maybe that would work with the castle too.

Eugenie thought that music was a better way to think about it. There was harmony—the things that seemed to go together like notes did, or odd numbers and even numbers in math. Things just seemed to belong in groups, and groups would help someone think about anything that was complicated. Patterns. If you knew the patterns, you could decide what fit and what didn't.

Alyssa shook her head. That was part of why she had wanted to leave the castle and go to become a gardener for the rest of her life. Gardening always made sense because you could always see the results. Strong and healthy plants? You know you did the right thing. A plant that didn't get enough sun would tell you that. Water and food, too. The plant would talk to you, it would say: wait, over here, fix this, too much shade. Alyssa had come to trust this way of knowing the world. Eugenie had delighted in her patterns and how patterns fit other patterns.

Jake had wandered back to where the girls discussed these important ways of thinking. Jake listened. Briefly he thought about adding his squirrel-sense to the talk. But he decided not now. The girls, he thought, were only missing the magic of him becoming a squirrel, the magic that somehow solved all the problems and jumped over all the difficulties and went right to the way a squirrel's tail automatically balanced its body on a thin branch. All the problems seemed already taken care of.

As the children thought their ways into the kingdom's difficulties, there appeared far off a cloud of smoke above the castle. Jake noticed it first and pointed to it wordlessly. Then Alyssa and Eugenie stopped talking and stared. The cloud began just above the trees that hid the castle from view. It looked like a wisp of cloud at first but kept growing, gray in the center and darker on the edges. It was round on the top but soon flattened out and grew fat edges that rose into the afternoon sky. In a short time, the cloud mushroomed so large that the clear, bright blue sky grew darker and darker. From where they looked, the cloud seemed like it would never stop growing until it ate the trees, ate the afternoon, ate the sky. They watched and could hear each other breathe.

Eugenie thought that a cloud of smoke was a breaking of order. Alyssa thought it looked like a weed. Jake just plain didn't like the way it sat on top of the trees as if the entire forest was on fire. And the only noise was the wind until in the distance and with a regular beat came a dull hammering like someone pounding the earth.

Chapter 12

Some birthday week! Jake thought. The cloud in the sky over the castle grew and grew until it swallowed a nine-year-old's birthday party. The road outside the farm was filled with carts and ragged people, and Jake's parents decided quickly that they would have the birthday party later. Jake thought: if there *is* a later.

The road was jammed with carts piled high with chairs and blankets, and in more than one case, children. The oxen plodded and must have wondered at this scruffy parade with no joy in it. And the weary spectacle dragged on and on. Jake had been forbidden to go out to the road. His parents wanted to find out what was happening before he was allowed to wander again. Rumors had already arrived that an explosion in the castle had killed some, injured many, and no one knew who did what. The King was still at least a day away with his troops chasing pirates. The Queen, they said, was nowhere to be seen.

But all this was rumor and parts of things that always began with, "Somebody said that…" Or, "I have a cousin who wasn't actually there but he heard…" And so Jake's family was going to be very careful. No matter what happened, there would be animals and fields to tend, chores to do, milk to sell and cheese to make. As in the past, the farmers held their breath and then found out what their new world was going to be like. The castle had one idea of history—what had happened to the families that counted. The farmers had a completely different history that had stories about where to hide the little money they had, how to nod and say yes and wait to see how the new leaders behaved themselves.

"At least with the pirates, you know what they want and

what they will do," Father said. "And they never invent a new tax and make you pay it after a war. They take two sheep and leave. Something very direct about it." He stood sharpening a sickle with long strokes of the whetting stone. In the distance, the smoke cloud had cleared but streams of gray haze blew back and forth in the skies over the castle. Alyssa was building a small scarecrow for her garden as if it might also keep away whatever was gnashing its teeth in the castle. Eugenie had not been heard from since the day in the garden. But Jake felt that Eugenie would find a way to do exactly what she wanted to. They might try to lock her up with her mother, but somehow, Jake knew, she would turn into a bird and fly from the window.

Jake thought more and more about escaping to the old couple's garden and begging them to let him be a squirrel again. In the trees there would be only wind and sun and the next branch. He could sit on his haunches and nibble anything he found, just to see if it was good to eat. The wind would be a story full of whispers here and whispers there. Cat. Black snake. Red fox. Dog. Another squirrel. So simple and full of the joy of being alive. No black clouds: neither the one in the sky nor the one he saw in his mother's eyes when she watched the carts drag by on the road.

Jake found Alyssa sitting in her own garden surrounded completely by tall pea vines and tomatoes that had been short plants before she sprinkled the soil around them. He could see her sitting in the dirt with her fingers poked into the soil as if she were trying to grow roots herself. He heard her sigh. Once she had told him how she envied plants, the beautiful way they lived on the earth. He thought she might be kidding him about his climbing trees. And she was just saying the opposite to annoy him; that's what he thought at first. But then he saw in her eyes a kind of faraway look he hadn't seen before. It certainly wasn't the look she used when she was kidding him. Did she really want to become a plant? Or just think about what it would be like. He thought about being a squirrel and how for the first few minutes he was a boy thinking how great it was to be a squirrel and then very soon the boy part faded, and he became all furry creature running the branches of the fine beech tree.

Alyssa noticed Jake and pulled her fingers from the soil and slipped on her work gloves. "Jake, what are you doing here? Don't you have chores?"

He pointed toward the road. "I can NOT go look, Mother says. I am NOT to go up in trees or climb the barn or—anything!"

Alyssa smiled. "But you CAN do work, can't you? Oh never mind. I know what she's thinking. She would hide us all in a hole in the ground if she had her way. When this business was all over, then we would come out and go about being a family. That's her way of saying she loves us, I guess."

"But what can we *do*?" Jake couldn't hide his frustration.

"We can only wait. Wait for Eugenie, for one thing. I know she'll escape somehow and come to us with news. Then we might be able to do something, but the way Father and Mother are talking about this whole business, I don't see how they'll let us do anything at all. Still…"

Jake waited for her to finish, but she didn't. She just sat in the dirt and looked up at him. The sun through the trees speckled the ground and Alyssa looked to Jake like she just might fade right into the dirt and be gone. He shook his head like he'd seen the horses do to flick off flies. She was back.

It was two days before Eugenie showed up again. She used her usual way: she had climbed to the back of the hayloft and whispered to Alyssa when she knew Father and Mother were elsewhere. Out of the dark shadows where owls slept away the day, where cats stalked mice, came her voice. And they were all together again, meeting at the edge of the old couple's garden.

Jake found it much easier to escape from the barnyard now that days had passed since the road had filled with people fleeing the castle. The smoke had cleared, and only a few carts passed headed away from the problems.

Eugenie went first. "The King and his soldiers, well, some of them, got back in time, I think. But the Soyle-Regolith group of families have the castle. I think some of the soldiers caught there might escape and join the King if they knew he was back, but they can't tell what's going on and no one will tell them. So they stay with the other side. I'm not exactly sure how many would go back to the King. But the Queen is in the castle locked in her rooms, I think. At least that's what the servants think. The servants will stay with whoever wins. I don't think they have a choice in the matter. So the next few days will be important. Everything depends on whether the soldiers in the castle choose the King or the other group. Wherever they go, there goes the kingdom. And both sides know it. The King's troops must be frantic to get word to the troops inside. And the Soyle-Regolith people are set on stopping it. If only we could get word somehow to the soldiers in the castle that the King needs them to restore the peace."

Alyssa scratched her head. "Maybe the King's men could use birds with messages."

"I saw marksmen on the castle walls shooting every flying thing that goes near. I think they probably tried that already. In a day or two more the King's troops will have to go find food. They'll go farm to farm taking what they need. But inside the castle, they probably stored up food before they blew up the Council Chamber."

Jake said quickly, "Oh, was that the smoke cloud?"

"Yes. The King's oldest councilors are prisoners now."

"How did you get out?" Alyssa asked.

Eugenie smiled and glanced at her. "You remember the gardener's entrance at the base of the back wall? They sealed that right away. But down the wall—you remember, near the back of kitchen wood box—I saw that someone had made a hole to the outside of the wall so wood could be put in the opening from the outside and then taken into the kitchen from the inside. One day I was curious how big the hole was. It was a small room, so they could put lots of wood in there. And the way to the outside was big enough to crawl out just around the corner from the gardener's entrance. There were spiders in there... Well, let me just say big enough for a small child to ride. This big!" And she held out her arms the size of a spider no one ever wanted to meet. "I don't know what they ate usually. Maybe mice or rats? Or small ponies. But anyway, that room was a place no one ever went. They dumped the wood in from the outside. They took it in the kitchen and piled it up for using in the stoves."

Jake was not fond of spiders, and he knew that Eugenie made the spider even bigger than it was, but just the same... Spiders were spiders even though Alyssa had carefully explained how valuable spiders were in her garden and even more valuable in the barn where they ate insects. Jake had noticed that the higher up a tree you climbed, the fewer spiders there were. Maybe the wind kept them away. Maybe not enough to eat up there. Whatever it was, there was another reason to spend as much time as possible in the tops of trees.

Alyssa was interested in more details of Eugenie's escape. "Weren't you locked in your rooms? How did you get to the kitchen to get out the hole?"

Eugenie straightened her cloak and brushed off a piece of straw. "People have to eat, no matter what. War or no war, people have to eat," as if that answered the question.

"But weren't they guarding you? Guarding Mother?"

"They kept everyone separate. That's how they planned it. They divided up the soldiers into the ones they were sure were on their side. I think they promised them land and riches or something. But the ones they weren't sure of were kept down below in the garrison rooms where they couldn't see out and no one was allowed in while they talked to the officers one by one. That's what I heard from the girl who brought me food. Each officer was bribed or promised something, and the soldiers were kept in the dark."

Across the garden there was a stirring behind a row of giant dahlias, and all three of the children turned to look at once. The old man appeared and then disappeared again as if he had popped out of hole and then back in again. They looked around for the old woman, but she was nowhere to be found. Maybe she was in the house. But the windows were dark. No smoke came from the chimney.

Eugenie said that she had never seen only the old man; they were always together. Alyssa guessed that she must be around somewhere, and they just can't see her. The garden seemed to have grown, moved out from the center somehow as if eating up all the space between the house and the woods. Alyssa picked up a handful of dirt and held it for a moment then looked at Jake. "It came from here, didn't it?"

Eugenie looked puzzled, and Alyssa explained the present she had received for Jake's birthday. "I know. I know," she said. "Presents are supposed to go the other way, but the old woman told Jake he had to give it away to get his present. I don't think I understand either. But my garden—you wouldn't believe the difference it made."

Jake held up one finger to signal he had something important to say to his sisters. "I have a way." The idea had just come to him. Sort of. It was, maybe, half an idea still looking for its other half. It was an idea that rose out of the garden, the magical dirt, and his memory of being a squirrel. It was an idea with fuzzy edges, but the longer he held his finger up and his sisters waited for him to finish, the clearer it became. The old couple held the key. The power they had over plants and dirt and forest creatures began to sound in Jake's head until all the different sounds blended together into one great ringing note. It was sublime. He had heard his mother use that word about putting the right flowers into the right vase the right way. All the pieces came together. Sublime.

"Sublime," Jake announced. And his sisters looked at each other puzzled. "Sublime," Jake repeated. "That's how it will work. The soldiers, the castle, and someone—something, anyway—that can come and go with messages to tell those soldiers in the dark what's really happening."

Jake was done and felt he had said everything he needed to say, but his sisters both poked him with an impatient finger and wanted more. More details: *who* could carry messages. "Not me," announced Eugenie. "Once was hard enough! And they'll lock me away like the others." And then, "Not me," said Alyssa, quietly. "They would have me in a second with my tanned skin and working hands."

They both looked at Jake, and he smiled. "Me," he offered. "Me, of course. I could get to the castle without touching the ground and then, go up a dark wall, across a roof, through a crack in the stones…"

Jake paused to let his sisters imagine with him. But only one, Alyssa, was following at all, and even she was not sure what she was hearing. Eugenie was shaking her head in that "my silly brother" way she always used when Jake's imagination got the better of him: ghosts, talking rabbits, flying cows. Jake had a history of flying off the earth into the sky of his imagination.

But Alyssa's eyes narrowed while she was assembling the pieces: Jake told her he had been a squirrel; the old couple had given the gift of magic dirt. She had believed only one of these, the one she saw with her own eyes. The squirrel part she had put away on a shelf in her brain where she kept Jake's nonsense talk. She found herself taking from the shelf the squirrel part.

"Jake, do you mean that you really could be a squirrel? For a while? How? For how long?"

"Wait," chimed in Eugenie. "I am not understanding one word of this squirrel business, I'm afraid."

And so Alyssa explained what Jake had told her, how she had shelved the information. And then she turned to Jake. "You weren't kidding, were you?"

"Nope." Jake waited for it sink in. Both girls— two princesses, two farm girls if you counted all the possibilities—took a deep breath together, and then let it out. "Jake!" they said both at the same time, in the same way. It was the way both had of telling Jake it was time to come clean and say it out clearly.

"Nope," Jake repeated, just to annoy them a little. But then quickly added, "I can be a squirrel. I can. I really can. Only…" And Jake rubbed his chin and stared off into space because he really didn't know exactly what to say next. He knew he had to come back when the old woman whistled, when either one whistled. He wasn't really sure who whistled. But he knew he had to come back or… Or what? He didn't exactly know what.

The girls waited. Jake continued, "Only I have to *mutatis*

mutandis." The words came to him from somewhere in his memory; he heard them as an echo from when he got changed into a squirrel or maybe when he changed back. Something changing, something that *has* to change before something else. It was foggy. But the words were clear: *mutatis mutandis.* The girls waited some more.

Jake told them as clearly as he could remember how they had gone into the woods, the tent of branches, the treetops, the whistle, the return. Oh, and the cookies. They were truly fine cookies. Alyssa and Eugenie waited until he had finished. Together they looked around the garden for the old couple, but there was no one.

Chapter 13

Eugenie and Alyssa were talking about whether going back into the castle was a good idea. They decided no. Getting out one time, maybe two, was just about knowing all the different ways the castle leaked its prisoners. But after that, the danger of getting caught meant that the guards would begin to fill all the escape holes. The servants might be beaten—or worse—for letting it happen, and the princess might even be chained. No one knew exactly what the Soyle-Regolith family was capable of. They had waited, not patiently, for several generations to return to what they considered their rightful place as king and queen of the kingdom. Now they must think themselves very close to making right what was wrong for all those years. Eugenie thought that their desperation had now become resolve. Alyssa nodded. Jake thought she should explain what that means. And so she did: the Soyle-Regolith family had put all their eggs into one basket. And now they would be fierce in protecting that basket. If they lost this chance, they would lose everything—name, wealth, position, power. Jake knew about the eggs-basket idea. He had once tripped—ironically on a tree root—and spilled an entire basket of newly collected eggs onto the ground. Half of them broke. More irony: the chickens rushed over to eat the broken ones. The dog came quickly too. Then Mother had taken the time to explain not putting all your eggs in one basket and how it meant more than just eggs, too. That sometimes people took a big chance and lost when they could have taken smaller chances, one at a time, and not lost everything if something went wrong. Eggs. Baskets. The Soyle-Regoliths, Jake imagined, had a heap of golden eggs in a giant basket in the castle, and now they were willing to do anything, anything at all, to protect their eggs. Even very mean things. Eugenie nodded. Even killing things. Both girls nodded. Even torturing things like... But the girls stopped him and said that, yes, yes and yes. The S-R family were capable of *anything,* anything you could imagine. Worse than pirates? Jake asked. Worse than pirates even, the girls responded. Sadly, yes. Worse than pirates, but none of them knew exactly what pirates actually did or even the actual things that were so bad they wouldn't talk about them. But all three agreed, BAD THINGS.

So, it was settled, in the way something tricky is settled. They would all three do whatever they could think of doing to help Eugenie's father and mother stay king and queen. They also knew Eugenie could not go back to the castle, she could not come live at the farm, and she could not wander the countryside. For the time being, she would have to live a little way into the woods, and Alyssa and Jake would have to bring her food and help her with blankets to stay warm. Then they could meet each day and gather their brains together and make plans and carry them out. Alyssa thought it would be nice if they knew of a cave where Eugenie could live, like in books. But there were no caves here. Only on the sea coast. And so she would have to live in the woods.

Pirates, it turned out, made all the difference. They had been so successful—a sheep here, a pig there—at gathering food, that miles from the coast they had set up a sort of market that was really just fences and pens to keep what they had stolen. They had so much stock from raids that they began to sell some of it to whomever would buy. They sold cheaply because they didn't have pastures to graze the sheep, no slops for the pigs. So what they couldn't immediately get to a ship, they bargained back to the people, even some of the people it had been stolen from. The King's men had just begun to chase the pirates back toward the coast when word arrived from the castle: war had begun. The Soyle-Regolith rebellion had begun. More than a hundred pirates had been trapped against the coast without their ships. The King's men were moving in to capture the pirates and set the stock loose when the word arrived, and all the King's horses and all the King's men... Well, we all know that part. They all turned toward the castle, several days away, and the pirates could be heard cheering as the troops left.

News traveled even faster than the King's troops. From town to town the word spread that the King was returning. There was no word from the castle, but the doors were sealed up tight, even a part of the road nearest the castle had been dug up and the holes filled with water so that mud was deep and discouraging.

Eugenie, the farm girl turned princess and now turned fugitive, tried to make herself comfortable in that part of the woods where she could not be seen by someone passing by, but not so deep in the woods that there was little day and no wind. The really big trees, the ones that had their own territory and shaded out the little ones too close to their immense trunks, those forest giants that seemed to live forever if the woodsman's axe spared them, those old ones that ruled the sun and earth, there Eugenie made her new home. The spring had nearly become summer but the nights remembered winter at times. She huddled in the blankets brought by Jake and Alyssa, but on a farm every blanket counted, every blanket had its use and place. So as not to become suspicious, Jake had taken the animal blankets first: the saddle pad for the riding horse, the paddock blanket, and one blanket from his own room. Alyssa found scraps and pieces of heavy cloth that would not be missed immediately, and she added her favorite sleeping blanket, the one with the very soft cotton edging that she kept close under her chin when she was going to sleep. All these made Eugenie's nest. She tucked and pushed every scrap they had brought her on top of a layer of leaves, another layer of pine boughs, and then wriggled herself into the nest to become warm. Going to sleep was warm enough. She was used to the forest noises; she even liked them. But in the early morning when the least heat had faded, her nest was not warm enough. The air moving over the forest floor seemed to sway in the first flickering of morning light. And that little willful wind made Eugenie shiver. She burrowed deeper as if the tree roots themselves might warm her. But no warmth came.

Soon it would be warm enough all night long. But not yet. When Jake came bringing bread and cheese, he noticed Eugenie looked very tired and more than a little unhappy.

"Are you? I mean, Eugenie, do you want me to? What can I do?" Jake said all in one quick string. He was watching her rub her eyes with the back of her hands. She coughed and coughed.

"I will be fine. When the nights are a little warmer, I'll be fine. It's just that now the cold kind of seeps into me at night. I can't get all the way warm." She coughed again.

"Are you getting sick? Should I bring some of Mother's tea she makes when we are sick? I could pretend it was me who..."

"No."

Jake thought she might want to be alone and said, "Alyssa will come later. She had to go help Mother take something somewhere. I didn't hear very well. She won't be too late." And Jake went a short way back toward the fields that came up to the edge of the woods. There he stopped and looked back. He could just see Eugenie fitting herself into a sunny spot and curling her back to the warm glow.

Jake had a feeling this was not going to work out at all. Something felt wobbly in the plan to keep the girls' secret. And then there was the castle mess. And then there were pirates he heard his parents discussing. What else? He felt so much like becoming a squirrel where none of this mess counted, that he could almost feel his whiskers and fluff his plump tail. The trees would be the place to be when all this business came together. Up high everything was elegant, even when some jay took offense at him being there and dove after him trying to snatch a piece of his tail. Even when he heard the whistle and ached to stay but knew he had promised to come back. The old woman had taken his face in her gentle hands and looked him in the eyes. Did he understand how important it was to return immediately? Was it completely clear that he *must* come back? She had said the same thing two different ways just to make sure. He had nodded. And then nodded again. She waited. Finally, he said, "Yes. Yes, I understand." And that was that.

Eugenie did not look very well after the second night. Her cough was worse. Jake and Alyssa thought that another night sleeping on the branches was not a good idea. Eugenie said she would be fine and went to nap during the afternoon warmth. But by evening, it was clear. She was getting worse. Alyssa sent Jake to find the old woman. Maybe she could make some potion that helped like their mother did. Herbs from the forest, tea, and, Jake suggested, maybe those cookies she always had in her apron. So Jake took off running.

The sun was still warm, Eugenie still napping, the whole spring world sliding into evening by the time Jake got back. The old woman was walking carefully behind him. She carried a small basket covered in a checkered cloth.

Alyssa walked quickly to greet them and not wake

Eugenie. "She's been sleeping. But she wakes a little to cough. It's a deep cough." And she tried to copy the cough for the old woman to hear.

The old woman drew closer to have a look at Eugenie, who stirred but didn't waken. "The difficult part is sometimes in not being sick, but in being separated."

The children looked at each other quizzically. "Separated?" Alyssa asked.

"Maybe there's a better word. Out of balance? Uncomfortable? But I like the old word, discombobulated. When too many little things seem to be just a bit wrong, and too many big things seem to be very wrong. They kind of add up, you know. Sometimes when part of the forest burns, it takes a long time to get back into balance again. The animals know and, if they can, go to another woods. If there is no other place to go, then they become uncomfortable all the day long. A kind of sickness, it is. One that takes time to fix. But in the meantime..."

Jake thought maybe Alyssa was understanding all this, and he would ask her later what the old woman meant. Then he looked up at Alyssa's face and realized that maybe she was not understanding either.

The old woman continued. "Sleeping in the woods, even getting cold, does not make people sick. It makes them unhappy sometimes. But becoming this kind of sick is something else. Her second family is in danger. Her first family is very close by, but she believes she cannot go to them. She is caught."

Eugenie stirred and coughed. Jake could see her open her eyes but not get up. She was listening.

Mrs. Trueblood reached into the basket and brought out not herbs and medicines but muffins. She presented one each to Jake and Alyssa. Then she leaned over and set one on the blanket where Eugenie could see it. "Eugenie.

You can go to your family again. They will make you well. Many things can change if you go to them."

Eugenie sat up. She was breathing slowly and deeply as if the air was hard to bring in, as if there was not enough of it. She coughed again. "But everything we wanted, everything..." And her voice trailed off. "I'm so tired. I can't find the place that makes me feel all the way awake. Everything we wanted. We both wanted. We worked very hard so both of us could find our way."

"And you did. You did find your way. But now think that everything is always changing and nothing holds still." Eugenie had nibbled her muffin and then began to eat it more quickly. Jake had finished his and was looking at Alyssa's where she held it in her hand and took small bites.

"Mrs. Trueblood? What will happen if I go home to see Mother?" Eugenie asked.

"I don't know. But more balance will happen, I think. And that is always good. You could find out. Just by walking over there." And she pointed over her shoulder. "Love is there. Love is a fine kind of balance. You could find out. And there are many things changing in the kingdom. In these times it is good for people to stick together. Things will happen but be easier if people are together."

Eugenie sat eating her muffin. She sighed. "We would have to change back..." She looked up at Alyssa. "Like we did before but that was just for a short while."

The old woman held up one finger. It was slightly bent and rough from working in the dirt. "There is another way," she said. "Another way to balance things."

All three children looked at her. Would she say something strange again that no one would understand? Something about trees or wind or mountains or some bird?

"There is an easy way. Both girls go home and stand

together. There are curious times coming, I can see. But both of you in the safety of the farm could just be what is right. Try it. There is great love there. At home. In the earth. I can feel it."

Eugenie coughed and Alyssa was worried. Eugenie should have had the pink cheeks of a princess. Instead she grew paler so that each afternoon in the woods as the sun slanted through the trees, the sunlight didn't seem to be able to find the princess. And each day the cough had grown deeper as if it came from a dank well somewhere inside her.

Alyssa took Eugenie's hand. "We'll do it, won't we? Go home to Mother and Father and get you well. Whatever happens will happen. We'll stand together through it all. And Jake is with us, and Mrs..." She turned to point at Mrs. Trueblood, but she was not there. Eugenie nodded; she could barely keep her eyes open.

Chapter 14

The homecoming was like a slow celebration parade. Eugenie, leaning on Alyssa, trailing Jake who carted the blankets and everything else they had taken to the woods, one pink blanket dragging and leaving a small snail's track in the dust, all came around the corner of the barn slowly revealing the tiny parade one thing at a time. Their mother was on the porch with her back turned. She poked spider webs from the porch corners and then turned and saw the girls, the boy, one of her blankets. She dropped her stick and just stood with her hands on her hips as if she were studying everything, but her mouth had dropped open.

Slowly, the barn now at their backs, the children came. Then Eugenie stopped and waved weakly at her mother. And her mother looked back and forth between the girls as if seeing them both for the first time. One was dressed as her daughter had been at breakfast, the other dressed in higher fashion but disguised somehow for the country. But the two faces! The pale one somehow just now looked more like her daughter, the face she nursed back from sickness many times before, that look, those cheeks, that wisp of hair. And those feverish eyes and the weak smile.

"In the house, girls," was all she said, and came to help Eugenie, who was really Alyssa again in her fever state.

Alyssa started to say, "We were…"

"Later. First things first. I think I see now. Explain later. Jake, go get some water to boil and light the stove. Alyssa, to bed." Both girls had suddenly become Alyssa. "And, Jake, after that, go get your father. He is in the far field. Tell him to come, now. Don't try to explain anything to him. Just say, 'come' and then you run back here."

The bed, Alyssa's bed, was made into a cocoon.

Water began boiling. And Father's boots could be heard clomping up onto the porch where he always took them off. Mother had made a tent and Alyssa was breathing in the steam from the boiling water poured into a large bowl. "Deep breaths," Mother repeated. "Deep breaths." Alyssa coughed with the first deep inhales. Then her mother dropped a packet of herbs into the bowl and poured more boiling water over them. The room filled with the sharp smell. The watching-Alyssa breathed deeply in sympathy with the Alyssa in the steam tent.

Jake was breathing hard from having run quickly back to the house. Father was coming up the stairs.

"Breathe," Mother said again. Then as Father's head appeared on the stairs, she pointed back and forth between the girls. "Two of them. Two Alyssas. Didn't we always say one was not enough? Well, now there are two."

Father came into the room and knelt by the sick girl's bed. He lifted the tent and Alyssa smiled weakly at him. He dropped the tent back into place and turned to examine the standing girl whom he had breakfasted with early this morning.

Mother said, "Amazing, isn't it? Without the two together, side by side—the tan skin, the haircut, the talk. We just went on thinking how quickly children change, how one day they look like an old aunt and then the next like a grandmother, and the next like—a princess! We live in extraordinary times."

"A princess? What? *That* princess? The one at the Beauregard wedding who made a speech and walked among the guests?"

The standing Alyssa raised one finger. "Um, no, that *was* the real princess. That was me. We decided to switch back just for the wedding because of all the relatives and the stories and the ceremony…"

"But you, Alyssa from the breakfast table this morning, you are the princess then?"

"Well, I haven't been a princess for more than a year. So I don't think of myself as a princess."

Father's eyes opened wide. "Until they all come and throw us in the dungeon for this—this business! Then you *are* the princess again."

Mother chanted her breathing instructions, Alyssa under the tent coughed again, Jake scratched his head (a little like a squirrel, in quick strokes with his fingernails), and then Mother stood up.

"Tom, we are in a new world now and everything we knew about the castle has changed." She pointed to the girls, "And this changes a few more things. Being thrown into the dungeon is probably the last thing we have to worry about—right after pirates and war."

Father nodded. "Pirates and war," he said, half to himself. "Pirates and war." And he stared at the standing Alyssa long and hard. Finally, he said, "How did my daughter..." He started over again. "How did a princess come to look... come to live under our roof? Where was I looking while all this took place? Jake, did you know anything."

The Alyssa without the cough came to Jake's rescue. "Father, we swore him to secrecy. I still don't know how he knew, but he did. Immediately. He knew and didn't tell because we asked him not to."

Jake tried to look as sweetly innocent as he knew how. He scratched his head again and wondered if he had caught fleas from his squirrel self.

Father and Mother stood together, and Father asked a single question: "Why?"

Mother added, "Was it supposed to be a joke of some kind? Were you playing a prank on everyone and it got out of hand."

"No." This came from the steam tent. And again, cough, cough, "No. It was never a joke."

And then the other Alyssa added her, "No. Not a joke. Serious. A serious chance we took to find the things we thought were the real selves. I mean, the real lives we wanted—one to the castle who wanted what was there, and the other here, to the farm where everything she loved was there every day."

Mother spoke slowly. "But, Alyssa, our daughter—oh, you're both our daughters by now—but the one we had as a baby, how could she leave us? How could she pretend each day to be a..." She took a deep breath, "A member of the royal family?"

From the tent: "Easier than you think. Everyone there is so preoccupied with being what they think they are, that anyone could jump in and pretend too."

And so the four of them, including Jake, began to tell what they thought about all this. Mother got more boiling water, more herbs. Finally, the coughing Eugenie stopped joining in from under the tent, put her head down and slept. The others tiptoed down the stairs and continued talking in the kitchen. Alyssa with her tanned princess-gardener cheeks tried to fill in wherever the questions went—the wedding flowers that turned into coins, the old couple's garden that resisted the King's men, the water problems, her own garden and love for dirt that loved her back.

All of this swirled around the living room. And when the swirling had ended, the family sat quietly and looked at each other. The big question of "What now" had not come up yet. Mother fixed tea for everyone, then went to listen to the breathing of the upstairs Alyssa.

Jake was thinking that squirrels never had to endure this kind of thing, this sitting around, this family of complicated people, this thinking about everything. But he decided after a short while that this complicated part was also very interesting. Pirates were interesting. Sisters changing places were certainly interesting. Father and Mother not knowing what was going on—that was interesting since all the rest of the time they knew everything. But they were just like children themselves when the two girls changed the rules of their world. And squirrels didn't have this much strange fun, he would bet. So, he thought he would be a squirrel in a second, just for fun, but always come back to this: family, talk, warm tea and muffins, a warm bed to sleep in.

The next day, his sister's cough was much better, looser and she had a smile on her face as she looked around the breakfast table at the gathered family. Father still had questions and doubts, but Mother seemed delighted, more every second, by the two Alyssas, the one Jake—the new crowd at her table.

And day by day the sick girl got well, just as the old woman had said. Jake did his chores then skittered off toward the old people's garden, but they were nowhere to be seen, so he returned wondering if he would get to be a squirrel again. He hadn't seen either of them since the old woman had disappeared in the woods and they had brought Eugenie home. Jake didn't know it, but the pirates and war and all that interesting stuff were gathering like rain clouds, and building deep and dark grays with trickles of lightning cracking open the world.

Chapter 15

The pirates, a small band of them with a wagon they had stolen from somewhere, appeared at the far edge of the field. The King's soldiers who had passed through the field a while before headed toward the castle. The soldiers were small in number because the rest of the soldiers were still trapped in the castle, and each day, their officers convinced more of them to come over to the side of the family Soyle-Regolith. Many soldiers resisted these new people and remained loyal to the King. Some officers, too. But each day in the castle a few more soldiers gave in and moved over to a room in the castle where the food was better, where there was more light from the big windows.

The morning dew had been heavy and left the grass around the field wet, and the small band of pirates made a clear track as they approached the farm. The sheep were in a far field, but Jake knew the ram would attack anyone who came toward them. That would buy some time. They would have to kill the ram before he stopped trying to butt them. Old George was his name. From when he was young George he would butt the dog, butt Alyssa, even butt Father. But as George grew older, he became dangerous. If you were not looking he could charge full speed and he would hit you anywhere he could. Once he had buckled Father's legs from behind and then stood over him victoriously. He would have crowed if he could have. The children were taught never to turn their backs on him.

Jake watched from the hayloft. He called down to Father what was happening—six or maybe seven men dressed in sailor clothing working through the tall grass toward the sheep.

"Jake," Father called to him. "Take the horse and ride

to see if you can catch the soldiers and tell them about the pirates. Be quick about it. I have to stay here in case they try to steal more than just sheep. Oh and, Jake, if you see any neighbors on the way, warn them too. Go! Bring the soldiers as fast as you can."

Jake felt his heart pound. If he could be a squirrel he could fly tree to tree and get to the soldiers in half the time. But the horse was in the barn, he didn't have to catch it, and he would have to settle for riding on the road. Before he left the loft window, he saw several pirates crash the fence posts and move toward the sheep with their stolen wagon. The trail of dew glistened like a snail trail. Jake hurried below.

He didn't bother with a saddle. He quickly bridled the horse and threw an old blanket across its back to sit more comfortably. Jake knew Old George would give him some time. He thought briefly about waiting to see how George would surprise those tough pirates, how he would pretend to be eating and then suddenly pick out the nearest target and charge. Maybe break a pirate leg. Maybe worse. The other sheep would mill around and corner themselves against the fences then suddenly break out in all directions. But he had no time.

The horse seemed to know how important this boy suddenly was. At Jake's slightest kick she flew out of the barnyard and down the road toward the marching soldiers. The road dirt flew up behind, and Jake held the horse close with his knees. He could see that the marching soldiers had taken a short cut across a field and they too left a wet scar in the damp grass. All these lines going to meet, thought Jake. But he could not take the short cut since the road would be faster. He could meet them as they came out of the edge of the woods on the far side, making his ride the long side of a triangle. Jake imagined Old George waiting,

waiting, choosing a victim.

Old George, as the pirates crossed the field, circled until he was between the intruders and his ladies. He could see only that they did not belong in his field. He began his foot shifting one and then the other like a small dance invisible in the grass. His head swung side to side a little at first, then more. His eyes were down, but he could see everything. And hear everything. The intruders came slowly. They had run into rams before, but they had not encountered Old George, or any ram quite like Old George. He waited. And danced.

The closest pirate had a long pole with a loop on the end. He had used it before to keep himself safe from crusty old rams. One of those rams was already lying dead in the wagon. He had slipped the noose over its head and then kept it from charging by keeping it off balance shoving it this way and then that so it couldn't get its proper footing to charge. Old George waited, saw the pole, the man.

Old George danced and waited as if he were grazing. Then he turned away from the man as if he had no interest in anything the man could be doing. Two steps closer, the pole slowly reaching out to slip the noose over George's horns. But just then Old George exploded sideways and in two leaps caught the pole the man had lowered to protect himself. But George, now not so old, plowed right through the pole, snapping it off and slowing him not a bit. He caught the pirate in the side of the leg and a second, deeper snap echoed the pole breaking. The man cried out and flew sideways grabbing his knee.

Old George did not stop to stand over his victim but had his second target well in sight. The second pirate turned to run, the long grass was slowing his feet as if he were running in sticky sand. But Old George had already chosen his target this time and butted the man's behind so hard he flew forward and landed on his head. George did not even slow down as he ran over the top of his second victim and headed toward a third. A nearby pirate fired his pistol, and the bullet hit George's shoulder but only made him madder.

Old George now had a scattering of targets, the shooter closest but others fanned out in the field. He chose the slowest one, the pirate leading the horse cart with the horse hopping off its front feet in fear, the man trying to hold him down. George was so enraged he charged directly at the cart wheel and crashed into it with a splintering of wooden spokes and a loud clang as the wheel came apart and the felloe iron ring sprang from wooden spoke splinters. But the wagon had dead sheep already in it, and its weight stopped George cold, stood him straight up as if he had run into a stone wall. George stood still for a second, then fell to his knees breathing huge snorts into the grass in front of him like dragon breath trying to burn down the world.

The scattered pirates regrouped away from the wagon. The shooter reloaded. Two others charged their pistols and fanned out to come at George from three sides. The destroyed wagon wheel had changed everything in their plans. They could no longer kill sheep and escape with the meat. They would have to drive the sheep in front of them until they could find a new wagon or drive the flock to the sea.

George got off his knees but stood breathing heavily in the same spot, the ruins of the wagon wheel scattered in front of him like bones. He was standing but not seeing anything yet. All his charging and butting machinery was stalled. He snorted and a long string of snot dangled from his nose for a second until he shook his head and flipped it over one ear like a pearl necklace won for valor. He began to see the men circling slowly toward him. They cocked their pistols—click, click, click. Each one eyed George, wondering which of them he would choose to charge. But George's feet didn't dance. His shoulder ached suddenly from the bullet stuck there in thick meat. Blood oozed down his heavy wool, a red badge. He saw all three of them at the same time.

A loud shot rang out as if all the pirates had fired simultaneously. But the pirates looked at each other. Not one had fired. And then, far across the field and out of the trees came two of the King's soldiers, then one more, then three more until about a dozen soldiers hurried toward the pirates. Without pausing the pirates turned and ran leaving their dead sheep, shattered wagon and snail-trails in the tall grass. Old George snorted again but did not have the energy to chase his fleeing enemies. And in any case, new enemies were making their way across his field, and he turned to face them, head down, feet beginning to dance again, just a little.

Jake followed well behind the soldiers where he had been told to stay in case the pirates began shooting. But now with the pirates running for their lives, the soldiers were running right toward Old George.

"Stop. Come back," Jake yelled, but his voice was lost in the wind and shouts of the soldiers. So he spurred his horse onward across the field to catch up.

"Wait. Old George. The ram. He will charge. Look. There he is."

The soldiers slowed, but Old George stood the ground between them and the fleeing pirates.

"Go around," Jake called. "Go around and he won't charge."

All the soldiers slowed but one, who didn't hear very well. On he charged, pistol waving, the pirates just disappearing into the trees ahead. The other men stopped, then called to their companion. But still he didn't hear and got closer and closer to Old George. Jake raced his horse past the stopped soldiers and toward the lone soldier about to meet George. Just as the ram's head lowered and the poor soldier noticed the wool and blood and snot on his right, Jake came riding between them and Old George stopped. He knew this horse, this noisy boy calling his name. And his pause was just long enough for Jake to steer the soldier away from George's fierce and wonderful valor. With Jake, the soldiers retreated. The pirates disappeared leaving their wreckage behind, their stolen sheep to be returned to the farmers they had been taken from.

But maybe more important than fleeing pirates, saved sheep, and brave Old George was that the soldiers returned with Jake to the farmhouse for water and rest. And there while talking with Jake, and drinking deeply from the well, they learned that Jake thought he could get in and out of the castle without getting caught, that he could take a message to the soldiers there and then get out without anyone knowing. The only thing was, they could not ask how. They could not tell Father or Mother. They had to trust that he could do it.

Chapter 16

The old soldier sat with his back against the well drinking slowly and saying nothing. He listened to Jake saying that he could find a way into the castle and take a message to the other soldiers there. He watched the younger soldiers look at each other as if to ask if they could believe this boy. How could he do that and they could not? Why would this farm child know things about the castle that only someone living there would know? One young soldier walked over to the long grass and spit as if to dismiss Jake's claim. Another rolled his eyes and said he would have to know exactly how this could be done.

Jake shook his head. "I can't tell you how. But I can do it. I really can. You have to give me a written message, roll it up very small, and then I will get it to the soldiers."

A tall, thin soldier patted Jake on the head. "That's a good thought. You're a good kid to want to help, but this is soldier business, after all. There are all kinds of dangers in the castle right now. We don't know exactly what is going on there. But we do know that the rebel family is getting our friends to change sides. And there are other risks." He patted Jake's head again. "Why, a kid could get killed in there and no one would know about. We hear the Queen and Princess Eugenie are held under guard. The King is beside himself with worry."

Jake said quietly, "I can do it. And if they did catch a child, what would they do? Not the same thing, I think, they would do to a caught soldier."

The oldest soldier raised his eyes to show he was listening, as if to say, "Tell me more."

The King and his close guard were sitting apart in the shade of the big maple, Jake's favorite lookout. The thin soldier looked over at them. "And there are not enough of us to get through the gate. Since we don't know who on the inside is on whose side, we could be in for a slaughter."

Jake said slowly, "But if you did know? If you did know how many of the others would help you? How important would that be? I could take a message in. *And* I could bring a message back to you. Just don't ask how. What do you have to lose?"

The old soldier grunted when he stood up. He refilled his cup from the well bucket. "Exactly," he said. "The only thing we have to lose would be this little guy here. We might never see him again. His people would miss him. End of that story." He paused and took a long drink. "A farm without a son to become the farmer when the father is old — that's a great shame."

Jake could not stop himself. He blurted, "But my sister is the farmer. She's the one who knows how to do everything. She's the one. She…"

The old soldier nodded. "I think that does make a difference." He laughed. "So it wouldn't matter very much whether you got back safely or not? Maybe we should ask your mother. And your father. Maybe even your sister."

"No. No," Jake said. "My sister can know, but not my mother and father. I told you I can do this. I can. But you have to trust me to do it. No questions. Just give me the message. Write on it what you want to know. I can get it there. I can."

Jake's enthusiasm seemed to catch on, even with the old soldier. He laughed, "So what's one small boy more or less in the grand scheme of things." But Jake could tell he was thinking hard about the idea.

The troops could wait a day or two more before approaching the castle. Maybe they could save a lot of blood if the boy did what he said he could. Maybe the kid knew ways in and out of the castle that no adult person did. It would be a shame if the kid got hurt or captured. But maybe even the Soyle-Regolith family wouldn't hurt a child. They could make sure he hid the message somewhere in his clothes or shoes, so if he got caught, it would seem like just a bad kid doing a bad thing. It would be easy just to make a message quickly, give it to the kid, let him have a try.

Jake watched while the old soldier drank water again and looked off in the distance considering all the possibilities. Pirates would not be a problem while the King's men were around the farm. The only thing he would have to do, Jake thought, is to find the old couple and convince them that a squirrel might be the way to save the castle from the rebellion. And I would be that squirrel, he thought. And I could never tell anybody, either. Just like when they let me run in the trees. A small collar, a way to fasten the message, a piece of hollow willow stem, that would be all he needed. Then tree to tree, up the castle wall, inside.

Then, the real problem. Get the soldiers to take the message. Somehow make them understand he could take a message back.

The old soldier called for pen and paper, then took it to the King's guard across the yard. Jake could hear the whispered conversation. There was nodding. The King stood up. There was more nodding. Several men gathered around and wrote the message. The old soldier came back and handed the message to Jake.

Jake pronounced seriously, "Tell no one. I will be back in a day. I won't be missed. I will leave tomorrow at sunrise. Not my family. Tell no one." And then he saw the soldiers were rolling their eyes again, looking at each other. "Please!" Jake said quietly. "One day. That's all I need."

And it was agreed. The soldiers would stay for one day at the farm. They would rest up for their assault on the castle—that's what they would tell Jake's family, while Jake did his work.

And Jake knew he had to meet with his sisters to find out about the ways he could scurry once he entered the castle. If he only had an idea where he was going in the complicated hallways and where the soldiers were being kept. They could help. But a problem arose immediately. Mother declared that tomorrow, Jake's birthday, would be a party. They had not forgotten. She would make a cake and share it with the soldiers the best she could with so many.

Jake thought fast. "But, Mother, couldn't we save my birthday? I mean, couldn't we just save it for another time. For just family. Yes. Now I have two sisters. I would like that so much better. We could be together, just family. Well, and one princess, of course." Mother looked out the kitchen window: the confusion of soldiers across the lawn, around the barn, settling in to the field, horses everywhere, the King under the tree.

"Oh, I had not thought about that. Maybe it would be better. There are so many of them—the soldiers. We could wait. If it was fine with you, Jake." She wiped her hands on her apron and gave Jake a hug. "That would be nice. Just us."

"And a cake. A big cake. Just for us," Jake added.

His mother was convinced. The birthday party was postponed.

Alyssa the sick, Alyssa the well—that was how Jake thought of them now. The sick one was getting stronger each time she slept and ate. Mother's tea, soup, toasted bread and jam, Jake knew the way it would go. He had been sick, and Mother had her ways. Always the same:

kiss his forehead to see how feverish he was, start with soup broth, add vegetables, the next day a little chicken. In between herbs and steamy tents and sleep. And more sleep.

Alyssa in bed was sleeping. The well-Alyssa sat with Jake explaining how the castle passageways were arranged: north-south passageways were laid out first in the oldest part of the castle; off these came the narrower passageways the servants took for most of their work; then the second building of the castle many years after the original had added new passages and, most important, hollow spaces where he could travel if he needed to. These hollows were made so the two different castles, built at different times, could expand and contract differently and not make great cracks. She explained that she had discovered these when she was still allowed to play with one of the serving girls before each had been required to know her place in the castle order. They used to explore these walls for hours if they could find ways to be left alone.

Alyssa made a map and took Jake through the old, then the new castle. She made wavy lines for the empty spaces. There were spiders, she said. But Jake had no fear of spiders. No great love, either. There might be a rat or two. Jake paused.

"How big a rat?"

It was an important question for Jake, Alyssa could see from the look on his face.

"Well, Jake. The really big rats don't last long in the castle. So the rats you might meet would be small rats. You see, there is a man and his son in the castle, and their only job is to catch rats. They have traps and snares and, well, all manner of machines and devices they invented. And they go every day and catch as many rats as they can. He is known by everyone as 'The Rat Man.' And his son is just

The Rat Man's son, poor boy. I don't think anyone knows his real name."

"Except his father and mother." This also seemed important to Jake.

"Of course. But one thing about The Rat Man is that you might run into some of these ways he has to catch and kill rats. It seems to me that a squirrel is really just a rat with a fancy tail, isn't it?"

Jake thought, no, no it's more than that. A squirrel flies around in a tree and a rat scurries in a sewer with all garbage and poop and… But he thought better of having this discussion just now with his sister. His sort of sister.

Jake memorized the map Alyssa had made. He traced it over and over with his finger until he knew where every little passageway led, which walls were hollow, which were solid. And where The Rat Man liked to set his traps. Especially that.

That evening, Jake slipped away from the great ado of soldiers and cooking and horses on the farm and made his way to the old couple's garden. There was light on in the cottage. He knocked on the door.

The old woman said, "Welcome, Jake," before the door was fully open. "Welcome. I was expecting you."

Jake explained his plan. She nodded. And nodded some more. But after hearing him out, she sat him down and again explained carefully and slowly what the rules were, what the rules *had* to be: he must return if he heard the whistle, he must always be careful not to fall and hurt himself because it would be difficult or impossible to help him, he must think like a squirrel and not like a boy. This last part was something new. Jake listened carefully.

She said, "If you begin to lose the squirrel thinking, you will find it hard to make the squirrel body do what it should do—run, be aware of difficult spots, sniff out danger. A boy will think too long. A squirrel knows what to do without thinking too much."

Jake thought that a number of problems were right there under his boy-nose, never mind any squirrel-nose he would have. Take a message to soldiers in a darkened room looking like a rat with a fancy tail. Be a squirrel in order to escape from anyone chasing him, but be a boy delivering a message. Come back when he was called no matter what he was doing. And then there was The Rat Man. And probably more and more and more.

Jake sat listening to the old woman, but his mind was running round and round like a squirrel being chased by a fox. The memorized map was hanging in his mind like a banner flapping in the wind of his thinking. It wouldn't hold still. The old woman tapped his knee.

"Jake? Do you want me to say all this again? Would a cookie help?"

It would. It did. The cookie she pulled from her apron was warm. And Jake thought that if he could just begin, all the complicated things would sort themselves out. Tomorrow he would be back at sunrise and everything that *would* happen, would happen. And some things he couldn't even imagine now, those would happen too. The cookie made everything seem possible.

Chapter 17

Jake woke even before Bester the rooster. Bester was fond of crowing just before the sun demanded it. Father had finally become used to Bester's early crow, had learned to sleep right through it. Bester never knew how close he had come to becoming dinner and being replaced. Jake dressed and waited with his shoes in hand. Bester crowed, and Jake was off, out the window down the slippery roof, across the barnyard. Pause. Shoes on. Scamper to the old couple's cottage. Sun just now cracking open the blue sky.

They were both up and about in their garden. Jake paused to see what they were doing, and they seemed to be just walking among the plants stopping here and there to touch one, lift another as if they might be greeting each one for the new day. The old man, who couldn't see well outside the garden, seemed to be able to see among his plants. He handled a tomato and tucked it into its stakes, straightened a flopping dahlia, lifted a squash vine into more sunlight.

Jake took a deep breath and ran into their garden where both greeted him as if he too were their special plant. He explained quickly, again, the castle problems, the soldiers, the needed message, his sisters, his family, Alyssa's recovery, the King's men—all in one long breath it seemed. A cookie appeared in the old woman's hand halfway through, and Jake took it but didn't stop even for one bite, just held it and kept going until everything was explained.

Finally, when all was said and Jake could not think of one thing to add, he took a big bite of the cookie and waited.

The old woman spoke. "There seem to be many

dangers—for a boy, for a squirrel. The way into the castle cannot be easy."

"Alyssa, both of them, gave me maps and directions," Jake said.

"But from the trees to the castle," added the old man. "I know there is a great empty space surrounding the castle. No trees, no bushes. Sometimes they take the hunting dogs there to exercise. A boy would be fine. Not a squirrel."

Jake asked if there might be a way he could go back and forth between boy and squirrel. Was there something he could learn in order to do it?

"I'm afraid not," the old woman said. She looked at her husband. Both then looked away as if some secret hung there in the air. "The changing is all very..." She looked for a word and found none. She tried again. "The changing must be done carefully. The changing to something else. And especially the changing back, you see. The changing back must be done, as we explained before, exactly after the whistle sounds. The time part is important. There is not much time between the calling and the coming, it seems, when everything is lined up properly. To make it all work. We know some part of it but not all." She sighed. "I suppose, in time, we will learn everything about it." She looked at the old man and he looked back at her, seeing her perfectly, and he smiled.

"We will," he said. "We will indeed. I believe we all will know all the parts of this mysterious thing."

Jake looked back and forth between them trying to figure out what they were talking about. Oh well, he thought. They seemed to know, he had trusted them completely when he became a squirrel, and he would trust them now.

Jake had the King's guard message rolled up tight in a hollow stem, very small in the hand of a boy but very large around the neck of a squirrel. The old woman went into the house and came out with a crocheted collar that could be fastened around a tiny squirrel neck. It looked too small for even a squirrel, but she assured Jake that much of a squirrel's neck was fur, and the collar would have to be fastened tight enough not to fall off on a mission through the tugging grass, the tree twigs, the tight spaces between leaves.

Jake thought a moment about when he was a squirrel—what he knew or thought about then. He knew he should listen for the whistle. That was important. But besides that he remembered feeling all squirrel, all jump and scamper and joy in moving among the leaves and branches. He couldn't recall thinking like a boy who had to do chores or be in some place at some time, who had to say please and thank you or go fetch his father a pail of cold drinking water from the well. He felt all whiskers and fur: hungry, alert to dangers, full of one purpose—being a squirrel.

This all skittered around Jake's brain, everything at the same time, in no order while some other part of him was itching, jumping up and down to get going without any more waiting. Everything would be fine if he could be a squirrel. He would figure it out. It would figure itself out. He would split himself between boy and squirrel and do what had to be done. It was more than just hope; it was believing he could. Be double. Be both and each.

Goodness, he thought. That was all thinking, and it was in the doing where he felt the strongest. Let's go. Let's do. Let's fly through trees and get this going.

The woods darkened along the path as they slowly made their way from the sun into the deep shade. The leaves above grew thicker until Jake felt as if he had entered a very large, dim room. They walked single file along a path only the old woman seemed to know—she in the lead, then Jake, then the old man keeping perfect step. Deeper and deeper into the woods they went, now deeper than before, it seemed to Jake. Why not here? Or here? But the old woman seemed to glide ahead without effort and seemed to know exactly where she was going. Again it occurred to Jake that the inside of these woods seemed so much bigger than the outside, impossible he knew, but a very real sense. He had been all around the outside of these woods many times—the part that came right up to their fields, the part that stretched to the road to the castle. But here inside it was like they were going to the moon and time stopped and the light belonged only to itself and not the sunshine.

Strange. But Jake had always loved strange. It was part of his love for tree climbing—the strangeness and constant change. Jake remembered the six-legged calf two years ago born on a neighboring farm. Father took him to see it. It hadn't lived very long or maybe the farmer took its life because it would have no life. He couldn't remember. But the strangeness of it, the marvel, the almost playfulness of being something completely different.

The path was no longer a path. Where the old woman led deeper and deeper into the forest was marked only by their passing, only by disturbed twigs and leaves crackling under foot, only by knowing that everything was about to change.

The birds were fewer and fewer and then none. Jake thought now more of a cave than a woods, but the trunks of the trees were now great stalks poking up like columns. A squirrel could appreciate how far around each was, how one could hide on the far side of so great a tree. And when they finally paused, it was to rest. The old man with a low grunt plunked down on a rock and rubbed his leg.

Jake had a thousand questions: why was it so far inside the woods but not outside? What exactly would happen if he couldn't get back when he heard the whistle? Are you two people completely magic folk? Your child that died, is he an animal here in the woods? Can I meet him? But he said none of these out loud. The silence was so deep, as if it were attached somehow to the darkness and their breathing all together here. It seemed best to be quiet too. And wait.

After a short rest, the old woman led off again taking a path only she could see. They walked slowly—a short and somber parade. Jake didn't know exactly how much time passed, only that he took many, many steps watching the old woman's back in front of him.

Then she said, "Here." And the old man sat again.

Jake looked around to see what was different here, what made her stop, but saw nothing different than any of the many twists and turns they had passed through. But she seemed sure. This was it.

"Rest a minute," she said, and handed Jake and her husband cookies. Jake looked for a rock like the one the old man found, but there was only the one. So he folded his legs under him and plunked down on the forest floor to wait. Wait for instructions. Wait for all this to begin his adventure, an adventure he only vaguely understood. He still didn't know how he would get the soldiers in the castle to take the message, read it, write something in return. Was that necessary? Was the message enough?

And just when the new round of questions was swirling in his head, the old woman said that now was the time. "And when you are travelling as a squirrel, Jake, go high in the biggest tree and you will see the best way to the castle. We will be here when you have to return. And the whistle. I do not, I think, have to explain the whistle again. Hear it. Come. Very simple. Do not wait. Come."

Jake nodded as if he understood everything, but what

he really knew is that he was happy to begin quickly now, and that, well, things would become clearer once he started. Soldiers, castles, trees, foxes, prisoners, even his two Alyssa sisters—all would become clear. It had better! Because at this moment he felt his heart tripping away inside him like the fluttering of leaves in the top of a tree in a wind storm. He was ready.

The old man grunted, stood and began gathering limbs to make the tent. Here in the deep woods it was more difficult because small branches were harder to find on the giant trees. But soon he had gathered an arm load and instructed Jake to sit on the rock where he had sat. One by one the branches were stacked like a cone around him until Jake could barely see out.

And as the light dimmed, Jake felt sleepy, but not in the bedtime way. He felt he was growing into the stack of branches, that there was no difference between him and them.

And then he was poised on a great tree, head up, then looking down at the two people just below him. He scampered up, and up and up. The trunk went on and then up out of the forest gloom into the light of the tree top. Jake felt no tiredness after his run up the tree, just the bright smell of high air moving through the branches. Then his head popped out on the farthest limb, and he could see the castle in the distance. From up here the forest did not look half as big as it did walking and walking through it. He could see all the edges clearly where the forest gave way to fields, and over there, a road, and in the distance a gray river that snaked its way through a small valley. Farmhouses, cattle, somewhere his own farm all lay below and tiny.

He pointed his black nose toward the castle and began to hop and prance his squirrel way through the treetops.

He could see where he needed to jump long before he got to the place, and he increased his speed just right to make the leap and fall gracefully to the thin branch of the new tree. On he rushed, his squirrel highway clear, the castle occasionally there in the distance, the leaves changing from tree to tree, all the questions that had busied his head now flown off somewhere in the wind. He thought for only a second of the words "follow your nose," and then those, too, were gone. And he followed his nose.

Toward the edge of the forest where the trees thinned and the largest ones had been cut down, Jake had to come toward the ground to catch a branch big enough to hold him. He could see the ground, the grasses, twigs and sticks, and then he was down with a final leap. In the trees he had felt invincible. On the ground was another story.

He looked left and right. And then again. And then he sat up, two paws under his chin, looking over the long grasses. It was a long and dangerous way on the ground between here and the castle. Far away a dog barked. What would be worse: a dog or a cat? Or a fox? Or some boy with a slingshot or a pointed stick with a may apple skewered on it ready to fling?

Jake made his way in hopping arcs like the boney bumps on the back of the old mare. Across the field, then stop. Listen. Something was behind, but far behind. Not very close. Maybe nothing. Hop again. This earth-bound business was not much fun compared to the delicious flying through treetops. The small collar he wore with its tiny tube fastened under his chin occasionally caught on the grass, so that when he came to an open field with a wheat crop just beginning, the going became much easier. But anyone could see him now racing through the young, green wheat seedlings.

Across the road, down the ditch. For the first time he was breathing hard, pulling the air into his lungs as if there was not enough air in all the outdoors and it had to be pulled from afar. He wanted to stop and catch his breath. Not here, but just ahead in the cattails growing on the far side of the ditch. He splashed through the shallow muddy water, resisted the urge to drink and rest, paused in the shelter of the reeds, and was startled by a blackbird that seemed to spur him on. The castle was not far, just over there, then up the west wall to the...

The map he had so clear in his mind was no longer so clear. His little squirrel brain seemed to be carrying a short version of it, all the nooks and crannies he had memorized now blurred together.

Jake-thought didn't matter. Squirrel power was better than a map. He sniffed the air for some other kind of map. Two quick scratches with his hind leg and he was out of the reeds and flashing toward the castle wall when he sensed the shadow off to one side, a shadow growing larger and larger by the second.

Hawk!

Chapter 18

Without thinking he dove down a hole just the right size for him. He knew tree squirrels did not go into ground holes, but the hawk shadow had nearly reached him. He did not stop to think about it but popped down the hole and waited. He hoped it was not a badger hole. He had seen a badger eat a ground squirrel, plunked on his mound and munching away. No, this hole was too small for a badger. A ground squirrel cousin, he hoped. And just a short visit. His father had tried to rid the pastures of ground squirrels because the horses would step in the holes and become lame. But Father's plans were not very successful. He would pour buckets of water into one of the holes, then wait at another hole to catch the digger. But more often than not, there was another hole and over there would pop out a fat ground squirrel that scurried away.

Jake turned around in the narrow tunnel, passing his own tail on the way. He poked his nose out. The hawk must have flown past, but he knew the hawk would not give up just because he had gone down a hole. A hawk was a patient thing and would choose a patient waiting place to watch.

A little farther away. He poked up both ears and head a little farther. Nothing. The castle wall was near. Time to run. Up the wall. If he could make it to the first balcony, then the great hall, and from there to the high beams... And then the plan grew blank. First the balcony and find a way inside.

The castle wall gave him great claw holds, the ancient slabs of stone heaped up with plenty of grabbing surfaces. And just as he rose toward the balcony, he felt the shadow again, felt it before he saw it, and then felt a searing sting

as one hawk claw found his haunch just as he reached
the shelter of the balcony railing. He hunkered into the
shadow and turned to see bright beads of blood welling
up in the slash. He quickly licked at the wound and his
nose became deep red with the blood. No time. Get inside.
Don't think. Danger. No time.

The squirrel and the boy in Jake jabbered back and forth;
he had become dual. He would need both if he was going to
get this thing done: boy for some parts, squirrel for others.
Jake slipped into a window crack barely big enough for a
sliver of wood. His squirrel bones seemed to melt in him
and move around and let him squish himself so small that
his whole furry self slipped through. Once again the hawk
shadow passed. Jake left a tiny smear on the crack where
his blood still tingled from the hawk's talon.

Down one short hallway, and there was the great room
with its high ceiling crossed by huge beams that provided
a perfect place to hide if you could get there. The soldiers
were kept far below in an assembling place about this same
size but dark and dank. Jake knew that to get below he had
to cross the great room and enter the hollow wall, then go
down. The rest of the map would come to him when he
needed it.

To get up the wall he slipped behind a large tapestry
that covered one wall. Like the one in the King's room, this
tapestry had battles and flags flying, soldiers large and
small in rows and scattered in the heat of battle. Jake ran
up the wall behind it brushing past loose threads in the
dark. At the top he peered out to see the assembled Soyle-
Regolith representatives gathered around several captains
of the guard who were cornered. Everyone was talking at
once. Not one person looked up.

Jake gathered himself and leaped the last three feet with
ease. His wounded haunch worked fine; the bleeding had

stopped, and he wore the red slit of courage like a badge on his gray fur. He was halfway across the large beam when he noticed a shape about his size coming toward him at a lope. As it drew closer Jake saw that this cousin had a plain tail, while he waved his fancy tail with every step. A rat!

The rat came nose to nose and stopped. Sniff. Sniff. It seemed to ask, "What have you been eating?" Jake let the sniffing continue, but gathered himself to fight for space on the beam. But then, just as suddenly, the rat stepped aside and scooched past and went on his way, having satisfied himself apparently that Jake was eating nothing of interest. Across the beam Jake went into the same hole the rat had come from—a hole high on the wall where two blocks had been put together poorly. Jake took a second to shake each paw free of the rich beam dust, and then slip into the dark and point his nose down. His crocheted collar held the message tube under his chin, but twice it caught in the narrow passage and Jake had to wiggle it sideways and work through. Down, and down again, and then down some more, Jake went blind in the dark but was guided by smells on this rat highway.

He suddenly remembered the rat catchers, the royal ratters. The traps would look like... Look like? He couldn't remember what Alyssa had said exactly. The traps would be... Where? He paused trying to remember. It was a shape. His squirrel-to-boy balance was swaying in him— clear idea, then all fur and nose. The traps would be set just outside the holes. That was it. Not what shape, but where. He had to be aware before sticking his nose out.

There was a small dot of light suddenly as Jake continued down. The dot grew bigger and suddenly Jake could see a little, then a little more. The inside of the wall was lined with fur stuck to the narrow passages from the many rats who had passed this way. And Jake could begin to hear voices, faint at first, then louder as the light grew. He stopped. The soldiers. Surely this would be the soldiers, and now he had to try to find a way to get one's attention and then get that soldier to take the message without first just seeing another rat. Now he could see plainly. He paused just inside the hole. He sniffed. Something smelled powerfully of humans. Was it only the room full of men milling and sweating? Probably. But, no. There was another smell. This one of old blood. Something just outside the entrance to the hole reeked of dried blood. The trap. Of course, that would be the perfect place for the trap.

Alyssa had made a model for Jake. She had seen The Rat Man make his snares, but they were no ordinary snares like the ones hunters used to catch rabbits. Those were a loop of wire that would pull closed just as the rabbit ran through. But The Rat Man had invented a better snare that began with the same loop and then added smaller loops set on the ground, and when the main loop began to close it would pull two other loops closed on the rat's legs too. She had made Jake the model out of yarn and explained the way the leg traps could catch a rat even if it only brushed through the big loop. And the one outside the hole had been very successful, it seemed. The blood of its victims still clung to the wires.

Jake listened to his own squirrel heart beating in his head like a parade drum rat-a-tat-tatting. Then he heard behind him a noise. He turned and saw a very small rat awaiting his turn at the exit. It was shy and stayed well back. Maybe a larger rat had snapped at it before. This was a half-rat, not much more than a mouse, really. Jake thought, a rat that size might be too small to become ensnared. Maybe it would. He would have to see. His squirrel thought was: "Better him than me." His boy thought was: "Too bad, but better him than me, and anyway, I have an important message to deliver, and aren't we all in this together?"

Jake hiked his tail up onto his back and made room for the small rat to pass. The rat waited as if to say, "No, after you." But very soon it crept slowly forward, and when it was clear that Jake was allowing it to go first, it hopped up to the hole and out. Then there was a rattle of wires, but when Jake looked out, the tiny rat was across the ceiling beam and on its way. And, more important, the snare wires were hopelessly tangled and not going to catch anything until they were reset properly.

Jake was out the hole and onto the beam in a flash. Now the hard part. He hopped to the far wall and paused. About three feet below him was a shelf holding lumps of something he couldn't identify. Then below that another shelf, and like steps down the wall, a final shelf about six feet above the floor. Without planning any further, Jake leaped to the first shelf, then quickly to the next and then to the third where he stopped and sat perfectly still on a lumpy bag of supplies. He made sure he was sideways, and his tail made perfectly clear that he was a squirrel and not a rat. He lifted his chin to show the collar and small message tube. And waited. Perfectly still. Then his tail twitched; he couldn't help it.

One soldier, taller than the others, saw him immediately. He said, "Well, what do we have here?" His friend saw where he pointed and said, "And look. It has a collar. With something tied to it."

"Easy, little guy," said the first, expecting that any moment this squirrel would bolt as squirrels always did. But Jake sat still except for his disobedient tail.

The tall soldier held out a piece of hard, old bread to Jake. He nibbled, and the soldier declared, "It must be tame."

Jake finished the hard bread and took a chance and

jumped right onto the soldier's shoulder and sat. The wide-eyed soldier said, "Look at me. Can you believe this?"

His friend proclaimed the tall soldier to be "The Great Squirrel Tamer," and more soldiers joined in the laughing. The raggedy crew looked to Jake like they could use something to laugh about. They were dirty and gaunt. They smelled of sweat and bad air and feet. Jake found it was all he could do to sit on the man's shoulder with his smell rising like clouds from a sewer. The shorter soldier reached up and removed Jake's collar, examined the tube, then poked out the tightly rolled message. He unrolled it carefully, unfolding and then unrolling again until he had the whole sheet of paper in his hand with its tiny creases and curls. He took it over to the best light they had and read it silently to himself. Halfway through he lifted his head and took a deep breath. "You will not believe this, men, but this is what many of us have been waiting for. The King and his men are outside the walls only waiting for us to join them. This squirrel must have been sent by the crown especially for us. Miracle of miracles. A trained squirrel from the King!" Then he put his head down again and finished reading the message.

The other men began to gather around and ask him questions. He explained the best he could. If what they wanted to know was not in the message, he shrugged. He said, "But one thing I do know, the King is waiting for us to break out and join him. How many have we lost already? They are picking us off one by one. Most of the officers have been taken and either convinced to join the Soyles or they have been killed if they would not join."

"You don't know that for sure," came from the crowd of men.

"No, not for sure. But the men taken out have not come back. Do you have a better explanation for it? I didn't think so."

All the while Jake sat on the shoulder taking it all in. The tall soldier seemed to enjoy having a furry friend perched there. The rest of the men discussed what they would do. *Please, please,* thought Jake. *I hope one of them is clever enough to think about sending a message back.*

And right then Jake heard the whistle. He was sure it was the old woman's whistle because he had heard it before, and it was so strange and high that no other sound in his life had even come close. And again, the whistle sounded long and high. He must go back the way he had come unless the men could let him out a different way.

The whistle again, this time like a one-note song pleading with him to come back and be a boy. Jake could hear the men too. A few of the leaders had begun a discussion about how best to make their escape, how to join up with the King before engaging the Soyle troops. They would have to run with their backs to the Soyle archers. They could be slaughtered fleeing, one man added. Others agreed. The discussion continued.

And Jake now heard the whistle as one long wail. He recalled the serious tone of the old woman's voice: Come back immediately; come back now. She had explained very clearly that if he disobeyed he would remain a squirrel. But Jake thought, *I have to stay until they have a message for the King. The King has to know they will join him against the Soyle rebellion.*

Time hung from the whistle like old moss. It was late. It was early. It was all whistle now in Jake's brain, so strident his tail twitched to try to shake some of the sound out of his head while he waited and waited for the men to figure out what they must do. They talked and talked; they smelled stronger and stronger; they huffed and puffed.

And in a while, Jake felt the whistle stop rather than heard it. It was like a weight leaving his body, and he breathed pure squirrel and waited. Finally, the men decided to trust this squirrel, write a message to the King, explain that they would await the King's signal and then execute their escape. They wrote and wrote until the back side of the same paper was filled. Then they tried to roll the paper small enough to get it into the tube, but it was too big. They tried again, and this time the paper was rolled tightly enough to fit. Carefully Jake's collar was refastened. Then the tall soldier gently picked up Jake and set him on the shelf. And there Jake sat, thinking he should have gone to the whistle. He didn't. That was bad. He should go to the whistle, but the whistle had stopped. He listened for the whistle. There was no whistle now.

Jake hopped up to the next higher shelf. The men's eyes were all on him. Then one suggested they lift him up to the one window with a crack in it, the one high above the floor. And the men made a ladder of one soldier on top of the next, with smaller and smaller soldiers toward the top. Jake saw what they were doing and leaped to the human ladder and scrambled up the fragrant backs of the men until sitting on the head of the topmost man who cracked the shabby glass of the window and then opened it. Jake jumped out and skittered down the wall into the long grass near the ditch.

Chapter 19

There was no whistle now, just the fine grass, the brilliant new smell of the land compared to the raw smell of the soldiers' room. Jake paused. Why go back at all, he asked himself? The old couple had assured him he would spend his life as a squirrel if he did not come back to the whistle. So, a squirrel it would be. Overall, maybe not a bad exchange. He was feeling quite good about being a squirrel, actually. But somewhere deep in his squirrel-thoughts there was the boy, the brother of two Alyssas, the son and farm boy and horse groomer and tree climber. But that voice seemed so distant that he could barely hear it, like someone speaking too far away against a high wind.

Around his neck, he remembered, was the reason for all of this exchanging hands for claws, a boy's tanned face for whiskers. The tube contained the connection he promised his sisters he would make—castle soldiers connected to the King's small army boarded in the fields around his parents' farm. Squirrel Jake and boy Jake wrestled in his brain as he paused to drink from the ditch, shook himself all over, quickly ran his paws over his face, tested his tail twitch and then set out across the open fields. Hawks hunted here, eyeing every movement; every movement meant a meal. Thin clouds decorated the sky like lace curtains letting most of the light through. Jake hopped and each time his back appeared above the grass it signaled to the hungry sky.

The small trees that began the forest were ahead, so far ahead it seemed, and so safe. Farther on the great trees of the deep forest were home and rest. Jake paused because he knew the same hawk that had given him the slash on his haunch would be the owner of this field. It was spring and there would be nestlings to feed and full-time hunting every daylight hour. The world was hungry in the spring; everything was eating and growing stronger.

Jake sat up and peered over the weeds. This last stretch had lower grass, some bare spots of dirt he would have to cross in a flash, then the tiny trees that would protect him from the sky but were the home of several foxes. As a boy, he had watched the foxes hunt in winter when he could see them pounce and spear the snow with their noses looking for traces of something to eat. The foxes also played, it seemed, rolling and nipping at each other in some kind of game. But now, like everything else moving or still, they would be hungry too.

Jake saw the shadow barreling across the grass at him. He didn't need to look up, he knew what was coming. And just as the shadow reached him, the talons lowered to spear his furry hide, he bolted to his left and heard the swish of feather and claw come up with only grass. Now, run! Run while the hawk collected herself to come again, while she whirled in the sky for the second, more deadly pass. The final patch of hard dirt was just a race for his life: nose down, long back legs fiercely hurling him forward, his whiskers plastered back by speed. And then the safety of the small trees, fox or no fox left to luck. His lucky day it seemed, and he flew toward the big trees and home.

The first truly large tree welcomed him with its great spreading beech branches that opened all the highways to other trees and the great giants of the deep forest where everything was as it should be. Jake breathed heavy and happy, all squirrel, the boy tucked away far down in the quick muscles that got him here. Higher, then higher again, then a place to rest and pant out his fear against the fine, smooth bark and the great umbrella of leaves above.

Alyssa and Alyssa—no princesses here on the farm—kept away from the soldiers camped all around waiting for orders. Both girls, the strong one and the recovering one, knew they looked too familiar to King and King's men and kept themselves upstairs. Mother too kept the curtains drawn, made sure the men had enough water, emptied her larder to feed them. And waited. She didn't know exactly for what, but she waited.

The girls knew what they were waiting for: a fine, gray squirrel with a message from the soldiers in the castle. Then he would appear as Jake the brave brother, Jake the hero maybe. Certainly Jake the tree swinger, the one who could soar where others feared to go. The girls, as the sick one became well minute by minute, planned to escape into the forest to wait for Jake. The old couple had told them that Jake would be changing back there in the deep center of the woods. And he would bring the message to them. But they couldn't wait and had to go themselves, they had decided, and greet their goofy hero.

But as they waited for evening and a chance to cross the farm unseen and enter the woods and wait, Jake came to them. They heard him before they saw him. The familiar gallop of a squirrel on the wooden shingles of the roof announced his coming. And there he sat in the window. Both girls turned to look.

A fine squirrel indeed, tail held high, proudly sitting on the windowsill with his frayed collar held together by the last thread of yarn, the small tube askew, about to fall off. Jake! They exclaimed at once. And to shush them, he boldly stepped through the open window, perched on the bed covers, and then curled up tail over nose as if he had been sleeping there all morning.

The girls looked at each other. Was this what the old woman said? He would come back as a squirrel? Then when would they get their brother back? The healthiest Alyssa carefully removed the message and unfolded it and read it. She would have to give this to Father to take to the King, but first it would have to be ironed flat to remove all the creases so the King would think the message had been smuggled out of the castle in some kind of imaginable way, not by squirrel. The sleeping squirrel breathed evenly, and they made him a better nest. They noticed the deep scratch and the dried blood caught in his fur. Sleep had so overtaken him that he didn't wake as they moved him and tucked him in.

The girls now had a number of problems to solve, and they had proven before they were good problem solvers: the kingdom's water supply, the challenges of switching identities, the new kindness of the King's rule. Now this squirrel brother, a trip to the old couple, the hiding out and sneaking around the troops everywhere called for boldness and thinking skill. The girls nodded to each other, and the one from the bed swung her feet out and tried out the floor. She was a little wobbly, but she would have to be the Alyssa at dinner, while the other one became the Alyssa who met with the old couple. They plotted in low voices while one very tired squirrel slept with his tail curled gracefully over his nose.

And in evening light, Alyssa milked, then threw down hay, then pretended to check her garden but quickly slipped behind the barn and was gone down the edge of the path toward the old couple's cottage. They were sitting on the stone bench waiting for her, eyes cast down. She sat, out of breath, and waited for them to speak.

"Jake did not come back in time. The only thing we asked of him. Maybe he could not come back. But the power wore down. I'm afraid the way to get him back passed, and now..." The old woman murmured so low that Alyssa could barely hear her.

The old man spoke louder. "We called and we called to him. The whistle. Something must have kept him from coming back. We made sure he knew the danger of not..." But he could not finish either. They both sat in silence.

Alyssa looked back and forth between their ancient faces now creased with grief. "Is there something you can do? *We* can do? Eugenie and I? Anyone?" Her voice got higher in a kind of panic seeing the old faces, before so certain and wise, now downcast and hopeless.

Two old heads shaking slowly. Then the old man and old woman together raised their eyes to each other and smiled. "It is time," they said at once, one voice that sounded old and young at the same time. "It *is* time," Mrs. Trueblood said to Mr. Trueblood.

Alyssa looked quickly back and forth between the smiles. If Jake was stuck as a squirrel, what had they to smile about? "Time for what," she asked.

But the old man stood up and walked a few feet away stiffly. Finally, he said, "Time is what will bring Jake back. Our time. His time. The King and his soldiers and their time. All the times can be made to come together, but we must be a little patient."

The old woman joined him. "One thing at a time, dear," and she looked first at Alyssa and then her husband. "But we both think the same thing. There is only one way left to get Jake back, but there is a cost."

"A piper to pay," he said.

"A reckoning."

"A long time coming."

They both said together, "A *long* and beautiful time coming," and laughed a conspirator's laugh, the laugh of secrets finally told and signs and portends revealed. *Their* laugh that belonged to no one but them.

They walked away from Alyssa together holding hands, leaving her sitting on the stone bench. Once around the garden they strolled without talking. Then back to Alyssa in the long shadows of evening. The sun seemed to wait and wait for them to make their walk around the flowers, the vegetables, the girl poised neatly on the bench.

They came slowly back and sat on each side of Alyssa. They explained that first the King must regain the castle: the soldiers, the Soyle-Regolith family, the just punishments— the return of order. They would stay in the cottage until all had come to pass. Jake's sacrifice and bravery must be honored in deeds and swift justice and mercy. And if these could be done, then there was one and only one way Jake could return to being a boy. The price of that magic was more sacrifice. The Truebloods, both of them, must be the sacrifice to give back a life. They explained to Alyssa that they were ready, more than ready, actually, to give all they had and were to return Jake. But the girls must carefully do what they are told to make it all happen in the right order.

"Timing," the old woman said. "It will be about the proper timing—our lives for his, in a way. But in a larger sense, we are not giving up lives so much as returning to the place of all life, while Jake will gain a second chance at his old life. Very complicated." She laughed. "Very complicated, and at the same time a very simple solution. Our time is run out. Our gift is a small one. Our energy just enough. Our love as great as any growing thing has. We will tell you how to make all this happen, how the pieces fit together, how energy and love and squirrels and old people and kings and queens and young girls and ancient trees all fit together." Her voice, which had begun old and creaky, had changed as she talked. It became clear and certain, beautiful and rich with purpose and direction. Still the sun refused to set, hanging on for the last word before plunging the evening into shadow.

Chapter 20

The King received the message from the castle without examining too closely how it had come, who had brought it. The instructions and signals were clear enough. His men were immediately put into action by the officers. The evening fires had just been lit when they were extinguished. The men mulled around gathering what they needed and making ready.

In darkness they marched past the old couple's cottage, past Alyssa hiding along the path until they were gone, past the dark woods. They waited outside the castle silently for morning light and the arranged signal.

Alyssa made her way home. The cottage light was out. The farm held one sleeping squirrel, one Alyssa resting in bed, Father and Mother who had begun to worry about Jake's absence, and the whole kingdom poised on the edge of a very sharp knife of possibilities.

"Jake is here with me," Alyssa called down to her mother.

"Fine. Just so he's home," her mother called back.

The second Alyssa arrived safely home, and two girls and a squirrel waited for morning.

By the dawn's light an uproar came from the direction of the castle. Smoke, faraway shouts, and clouds of dust all morning, and then quiet. Some short and fierce event took place, and all the land waited to see how they would be ruled, what songs would be sung, what tapestries woven with what colors and what victories celebrated. The battle as seen from the farm was very short and intense. And, most important, it did not include soldiers running through villages and farms destroying things.

Word came that afternoon. The King and his men were joined by a stream of soldiers from the inside and then others who stayed inside helped make the fight a very short one. The Soyle-Regolith family and the rebelling officers were now kept where the soldiers had been. The smell must have been unpleasant for them all. Justice was promised, retribution avoided if each would pledge in good faith to the King and Queen. A High Court was established to make sure of orderly proceedings for all.

And on the farm, one girl slipped away, another felt strong enough to try a few chores. And in her gardening clothes, she carried a recently awoken squirrel whose bright eyes shone through a button hole, and the tip of his tail poked proudly through the flap of her jerkin.

Jake, now the squirrel overwhelming him, breathed easy in his fur coat. The feeling that he should keep the boy-Jake in mind was all fading quickly. Every second that passed, he seemed to care less about returning at all. The entire squirrel business was becoming very comfortable, like an old coat. Mother, Father, those girls—what were their complicated names again?—all seemed to be far away now, in a room that grew darker and darker.

Jake thought there was nothing about being a boy that called to him anymore. He tried hard to remember why it was so good to be a boy, but he couldn't find the reasons. There must have been some very good ones, but now, whatever they were, they floated away. He seemed to remember something about a birthday party, one that didn't happen. Ice cream. Something else. Ice cream. And a tangled-up ball of parts of things and broken threads wrapped together, all having something to do with the name, Jake.

"Jake. Jake." He could hear Alyssa's voice, but nothing

in her voice seemed very important. "We have to go to them. We have to hurry."

But Jake felt no hurry. He was tired. Very tired. And Jake was finding himself very happy in that place just before sleep, the warm and safe place. *The nest,* he thought. *I am in a safe nest here. All is fine. So tired.*

And Jake slept.

Both Alyssas slipped away the next day. Neighbors had arrived at the farm with news of the castle battle. The order was restored. There would be peace and time to tend crops and animals. There would be market fairs in the village. Children could play, news be shared, and the sun would shine again, they all said.

The girls found the old couple sitting on the stone bench in the middle of the full glory of their garden. They seemed to glow right along with the great dahlia heads nodding over them, their pea pods already summer glorious, and the song of garden green was everywhere. They watched the girls come toward them and smiled to each other. Jake slept, warm against Alyssa's side.

"He's asleep, I think," Alyssa said. "He seems perfectly healthy. The scratch is healing. He…"

Both girls looked anxiously to the old couple for some sign, some assurance that their brother would come back.

"Come," the old woman said. "We have some work to do first."

And off they went, the old woman in the lead, like a slow parade. She led them three times around the garden. Alyssa, or was it Eugenie, doesn't matter which, began to ask a question, but the old man shushed her. Just wait, he seemed to say. Work to do.

And the third time around the garden, as if they had gathered from it what was needed, the old woman led them into the woods. She walked slowly as if choosing each step carefully, as if each place she put down her foot were an important place, a necessary step. To Alyssa it seemed almost like a dance she was doing. Right foot, left foot, wait. Right foot.

Slowly they entered the woods following an old path at first, but very quickly no path and then crackling through the fallen sticks and dried leaves. The dance went on, the parade went on, the old woman began to hum. Very quietly at first, so the girls did not hear when she actually began. But then louder and clearer as they made their way deeper into the shadows. The sun poked through the canopy only here and there, but, as if to make up for the lack of light, the old woman's humming grew louder. Then the old man joined in, he walking behind the girls so that they were sandwiched in the melody from in front and the deep droning of the old man behind. They looked at each other, and either of them alone would have been afraid of this strange song that was more like a chant that repeated and repeated. But together they felt perfectly safe no matter how weird the circumstances would get. And still, Jake slept in the perfect peace of a squirrel in its nest.

The old woman stopped walking but kept humming. Was she listening too? She cocked her head as if listening for some response to her song. They all waited in the darkness. One bird sang far away. Was she waiting for that bird? They began to move again. The deep dark shadows began to get brighter as if a new light were finding its way in from somewhere, from the forest floor this time, from the trees themselves.

On they went. And soon the girls could see that they were approaching a small clearing in the forest. On the far side there were great trees again and deep shadows. But they came out into bright sun and wildflowers throughout the grasses as if a giant hand had scattered them in various colors. Bright pink in one throw, yellow over near the edge, then tall blue larkspurs lording it over the center, tiny white twinflowers like foam on the green sea. Jake stirred and then slept again.

The old woman said only one word: "Here."

The old man immediately sat on a low rock and rubbed his sore leg. "Give me Jake, now," he said. And Alyssa carefully took the still sleeping Jake and placed him in his squirrel curl, tail over his nose, into the old man's hands. The old woman asked the girls to come with her to gather branches, and rather than cutting them from trees, she showed the girls how to pick the branches as if they were flowers, plucking them in one quick motion from the trees. Alyssa thought that it seemed the trees were handing their branches to the old woman, so she tried, and the branches came away with the slightest tug.

When the three of them had gathered enough, the old woman showed the girls how to weave branch into branch to make a kind of small hut with an opening on one end so that the sunlight streamed in. The Truebloods then smiled at each other, and without a word crawled into hut with Jake sleeping in the old man's large hands. The girls, not knowing what to do, waited until the old ones were both in the hut and then thought maybe they should go in too. But the old woman waved her hand to keep them out. Then she waved again, a kind of goodbye wave, Alyssa thought, then motioned for the girls to close the opening with branches.

With a few branches the hut was complete and the girls looked to see if between the cracks they could see what was going on inside. But nothing moved; they couldn't see in. They stepped back to wait for instructions, but there came no sound, no bird, no voice. And so they both sat down to wait.

The two girls, princess and farm girl, who had done amazing things together and apart, now plunked themselves in this beautiful place, and the smell of honeysuckle came from across the clearing. First one, then the other put her head down to wait and stare up at the sky. Then first one, then the other, fell asleep in the warm sun surrounded by the flowers the sun had made there.

They woke up together, too. The sun was lower, just above the trees, and pausing as it had the day in the garden. Inside the hut there was a rustling. And a grunt. Then a snore, and another grunt.

The girls looked at each other hoping the other one would know what to do. But the noises grew louder now, and knowing what to do was out of the question. Then, on the opposite end from where the opening had been, the rustling grew loud and then Jake's head poked out and peered into the clearing as if looking for something. Then he saw the girls and quickly pulled his head back in and announced, "I don't have any clothes on. Wait a minute. Here are some. Sort of." More rustling, the girls poised with eyes wide open, and Jake emerged wrapped in the old man's jacket. "Well, what are you two doing here?" he asked, as if he were surprised to see them so far from home. He yawned. "How long have I been asleep?"

The girls made sure Jake was fine—no squirrel tail, no pointy ears, no claws. Then they hurried to open the hut completely so they could see in. There were no old people, just their clothes. The grass and flowers were barely mussed as if only Jake had been in there. Alyssa quickly looked at the grass of the field to see if there were tracks, bent grass, broken flowers. None. Jake was back; the old people were gone. Everything was changed. Everything back the same.

And suddenly, as they stood wondering, one of them said, "Do you know the way back?"

And the girls began to discuss how to make their way quickly toward the farm. The opposite way of the setting sun, suggested Alyssa. And the other Alyssa agreed. Jake scratched behind one ear, very like a squirrel. Both girls stopped to stare as if he might begin to change back. But he scratched the other ear then, and they decided that they should move now before the light was lost.

The trail back through the woods seemed oddly much shorter than the walk in. And just as they left the woods behind and headed to the farm, the sun made up for its pause and scurried into evening as if it had waited to see them safely home. Jake was strangely quiet as if he were seeing his surroundings for the first time. The girls stashed him in the barn so they could get some clothes for him and pretend to Mother and Father that the three of them had just returned from an ordinary afternoon of ordinary doings. The Alyssa who like milking cows, milked. The other one scurried back from the house with Jake's clothes. Father was in the far field mending fences broken by the King's troops. Mother seemed unaware they had been gone. Jake confessed to being still a little tired and stretched out in the hay for a short nap before dinner.

And now that the family knew everything about the girls—well, almost everything—both Alyssas thought they should let Mother and Father in on their plans to each go back to the place they wanted to be. Eugenie—whichever one she was by this time—would take the castle and its classes and ceremony and protocols. Alyssa—the other one—would tend to her garden with its powerful new soil, a gift from Jake and the old couple. The girls announced at dinner that they would not switch back and forth very often. Not *very* often, but when the kingdom needed it, they would do what they believed needed to be done.

Mother announced at dinner that tomorrow would be Jake's birthday party—late. During the tiny war, the troops, the mess in the kingdom—there had been no time for a proper party. And it would be tomorrow. And there would be ice cream. And a kind of cake that could be made with what food that was left after the hungry soldiers had eaten everything they could find. Tomorrow, very early, all the children should go to the old couple's house to see if they would come to the party too.

And so they did. The girls and Jake made their way down the path, through the small woods, next to the big woods and to the old couple's garden. Of course, there was no one there. The cottage closed tight and looking very old itself, paint faded, the door hinge slightly askew. But the garden! The entire garden was invaded by creatures large and small. Rabbits and deer nibbled and chomped. Mice and moles cavorted in among the squashes where they had made holes in the biggest ones to get at the seeds. Two bright red dragonflies presided over all this feeding, perched on top of the highest posts that held up the vines of the climbing beans. Among the stalks sat two fox kits carefully picking off the young beans to eat. The children took in the scene. There was an eating joy everywhere and the deer and fox and mouse all ate together.

The dragonflies sunned themselves while the children carefully walked around the garden to see what other manner of critters had come to the banquet. And when they decided to leave, the two red dragonflies took off together and flew over the trailing Jake, came down in perfect precision and—for just a second, no longer than it takes to push back a wisp of hair—they alighted on his head. Then they took off together and rose up toward the sun.

**OUR STREET
BOOKS**

JUVENILE FICTION, NON-FICTION, PARENTING

Our Street Books are for children of all ages, delivering a potent
mix of fantastic, rip-roaring adventure and fantasy stories to excite
the imagination; spiritual fiction to help the mind and the heart;
humorous stories to make the funny bone grow; historical tales to
evolve interest; and all manner of subjects that stretch
imagination, grab attention, inform, inspire and keep the pages
turning. Our subjects include Non-fiction and Fiction, Fantasy and
Science Fiction, Religious, Spiritual, Historical, Adventure, Social
Issues, Humour, Folk Tales and more.
If you have enjoyed this book, why not tell other readers by
posting a review on your preferred book site.

Recent bestsellers from Our Street Books are:

Relax Kids: Aladdin's Magic Carpet
Marneta Viegas
Let Snow White, the Wizard of Oz and other fairytale characters
show you and your child how to meditate and relax. Meditations
for young children aged 5 and up.
Paperback: 978-1-78279-869-9 Hardcover: 978-1-90381-666-0

Wonderful Earth
An interactive book for hours of fun learning
Mick Inkpen, Nick Butterworth
An interactive Creation story: Lift the flap, turn the wheel, look in
the mirror, and more.
Hardcover: 978-1-84694-314-0

Boring Bible: Super Son Series 1
Andy Robb
Find out about angels, sin and the Super Son of God.
Paperback: 978-1-84694-386-7

Jonah and the Last Great Dragon
Legend of the Heart Eaters
M.E. Holley
When legendary creatures invade our world, only dragon-fire can
destroy them; and Jonah alone can control the Great Dragon.
Paperback: 978-1-78099-541-0 ebook: 978-1-78099-542-7

Little Prayers Series: Classic Children's Prayers
Alan and Linda Parry
Traditional prayers told by your child's favourite creatures.
Hardcover: 978-1-84694-449-9

Magnificent Me, Magnificent You – The Grand Canyon
Dawattie Basdeo, Angela Cutler
A treasure filled story of discovery with a range of inspiring fun
exercises, activities, songs and games for children aged 6 to 11.
Paperback: 978-1-78279-819-4

Q is for Question
An ABC of Philosophy
Tiffany Poirier
An illustrated non-fiction philosophy book to help children aged
8 to 11 discover, debate and articulate thought-provoking, open-
ended questions about existence, free will and happiness.
Hardcover: 978-1-84694-183-2

Relax Kids: How to be Happy
52 positive activities for children
Marneta Viegas
Fun activities to bring the family together.
Paperback: 978-1-78279-162-1

Rise of the Shadow Stealers
The Firebird Chronicles
Daniel Ingram-Brown
Memories are going missing. Can Fletcher and Scoop unearth
their own lost history and save the Storyteller's treasure from the
shadows?
Paperback: 978-1-78099-694-3 ebook: 978-1-78099-693-6

Readers of ebooks can buy or view any of these bestsellers by clicking on the live link in the title. Most titles are published in paperback and as an ebook. Paperbacks are available in traditional bookshops. Both print and ebook formats are available online.

Find more titles and sign up to our readers' newsletter at http://www.johnhuntpublishing.com/children-and-young-adult
Follow us on Facebook at https://www.facebook.com/JHPChildren
and Twitter at https://twitter.com/JHPChildren